forsaken
CONTROL

Cathy—
love doesn't have to
be perfect, to be
beautiful!

♥ Sapphire
Knight

forsaken CONTROL

an OATH KEEPERS MC novel

5

SAPPHIRE KNIGHT

forsaken CONTROL

warning

This novel includes graphic language and adult situations.

It may be offensive to some readers and includes situations that may be hotspots for certain individuals.

This book is intended for adults 18 and older.

This work is fictional. The story is meant to entertain the reader and may not always be completely accurate.

Any reproduction of these works without Author Sapphire Knight's written consent is pirating and will be punished to the fullest extent.

Dedicated to

my grandmother

You will never get to read my books,
But if you had,
I hope I would have made you proud.

common terms and names

MC - Motorcycle Club

Prez - President

VP - Vice President

SAA - Sgt. at Arms

Ol' Lady - Significant Other

Chapel - Place Where Church is Held

Church - MC Meeting

Ares - VP - The Butcher

Silas - SAA - 2 Piece

ARES

I WATCH HER LAUGHING AS HE PUSHES HER ON THE SWING. She's always happy, smiling, and just beautiful. He's lucky he has her. Is it wrong that I watch him too? That I find him just as beautiful as I do her? He shouts something to her, and she giggles unabashedly; he smiles widely at her and radiates happiness.

I want to feel like that. I want happiness too.

Her soft auburn waves blow in the breeze, giving me a full view of her sun-kissed skin. Whether I'm caressing it softly or grabbing it forcefully, I know it's soft. I've felt it glide through my fingers several times.

She was scared of me at first. I'm assuming because I'm not very friendly. How can I be friendly though? I'm the Enforcer. I'm meant to be mean, rough, and take care of things for the club. I love my job and my club; it's my perfect fit.

Now that we've spoken, she's not afraid of me anymore. She smiles and sometimes giggles when she passes by me. I love hearing her laugh; it brings me peace. I can't help but chuckle or grin each time.

He's been my friend for years and has never known that I'm attracted to him. I would do anything for him if he were to ask, but he never does. He thinks I like to watch a woman with him, when in reality, I only like watching him.

Now though...now he has her, and I want them both. I've never felt so torn before. I don't want them for just a fuck. I've had them for that. Not him completely, but we've been close. I dream of grasping his hair and thrusting into him roughly while I kiss her mouth. I doubt that fantasy will ever come true though.

She catches me watching them and flashes a bright smile, excitedly waving her hand at me. I grin and give her a slight wave back. He glances at me and smirks. He knows I like her, just not how much. He would probably kill me if he were to learn that they both own my heart. I wish I would have said something when they first started, then maybe I could at least have part of her too.

There's no telling what he or anyone in my club would say if they knew I find guys just as sexy as I do women. I don't generally give a fuck what anyone thinks, but I do value my brothers' opinions.

"You good, bro?" Cain comes to stand next to me, watching me as I gaze at them.

Blinking, I turn to him. "Yeah, I'm cool, man. Just enjoyin' this nice ass weather. You should bring your kid out." Cain is the one I'm closest to in the MC. He should be getting patched as an Enforcer soon also. It'll be nice sharing that title with him.

"Naw, London was talkin' bout givin' him a haircut and shit. She'll be here for the BBQ tomorrow though."

Nodding, I move my head to the side, popping the sore muscles in my neck. Fucking shitty sleep. "She's a fine ol' lady."

"Fuckin' right. Best bitch I ever met. What's up with them?" Cain nods toward the swings we had put in for the families. We say it's for them, but we all know the brothers really ordered the swings for Jamison, Cain's son. That kid is spoiled something fierce around here.

"Not a thing." Shrugging, I lift my chin toward them. "She wanted to swing, and he's wrapped around her finger."

"Yeah, that'll do it. I swear, London don't know some of the shit she could get me to do if she wanted." I nod, pretending to know what he means, when in reality no woman has ever had me like that. He claps me on the back. "It'll happen for you too, bro. Just give it time. It seems to be in the air lately."

No shit. Our crazy brother Twist, is busy following 2 Piece's sister, Sadie, around like a dog in heat. If she wasn't already knocked up, I'd swear she would be by him. There are more females around here than there ever has been before. I'm happy for everyone, honestly, but it would just be fuckin' nice if that shit happened to me too.

"I'm cool, man."

"Good. Well, Prez wants to talk to us 'bout some shit."

"He tell you what the fuck about?"

"Naw, man. You're the one he trusts over anybody else."

"Cain, your ass is gonna be an Enforcer before you know it." I smack his shoulder. "I'll enjoy sharin' the patch."

"I can't wait, bro."

"Let's see what the old man wants before he starts yellin' an' shit."

Cain grins and nods, following me into the clubhouse.

We stop outside of the office, and I peek my head in through the open doorway.

"Prez?" I call out and glance around the room, but it appears empty.

"Yep! Down here," he grumbles.

Entering the small room, I walk closer to his desk with Cain following suit. I peer over the desk because that's where his voice came from. He's lying on the ground, sprawled out with his long blond mop of hair in every direction as if he just woke up.

"Prez? Whats goin' on?" I huff, shooting him a baffled look, instantly thinking he's hurt or something.

"I need y'all's help. Come over here." He gestures as Cain and I shuffle around his office chair, coming closer. I glance down at him puzzled. Has Prez lost his mind?

"Get down here, damn it!" He growls and we both bend down next to him. "There's a safe under here, but I can't get this fuckin' carpet to move an' I was tryin' not to cut it up," he says quietly, gesturing under his desk at the old, thin carpet. "I know everyone thinks the floors are all concrete an' shit, but I had a safe put in. That's what this ugly fuckin' rug's about."

Cain starts chuckling, and after a beat, I join in. He must feel as relieved as I do. "Prez, gotta admit, you had me wonderin' what the fuck you were up to for a sec," Cain chortles out, and I nod, agreeing with him.

"Me too," I reply gruffly, grinning.

"You guys both are gonna make me stroke the fuck out. Now give me a hand."

I stand back up and Cain mimics me; grasping one side of the desk, he follows suit. We move it across the room and Prez is able to finally get the carpet peeled back. He obviously wanted us for our muscle. I know he trusts me a lot to let me in on the secret safe, but he must be gaining confidence in Cain as well.

"Prez, maybe it's time for a different carpet. That shit's fuckin' rank," Cain mutters, scrunching his nose up in disgust.

"It's just crispy from all the bitches I've had bent over on it."

I shake my head and roll my eyes while Cain bursts out in a belly laugh. Prez never has any females in here. The man might as well be a saint in that department.

"More like you ate too many fuckin' nachos and that's leftover sour cream," I mumble and nod at the floor. Prez chuckles and shakes his head agreeing with me. "Is that all you needed us for, Prez?"

"Naw, both of you come back over here. I wanna show you where this shit is 'case sumthin' ever happens to me."

Cain and I shuffle closer. Prez is bent over a decent sized hole in the floor.

"What the fuck would be happenin' to you?" Cain voices the same thoughts coursing through *my* mind.

Prez is the closest thing I have to family besides my MC brothers. The bastard who raised me is no longer 'round, thank fuck. The no good piece of shit who was supposed to be my mother got what was comin' to her too.

"Ares, you okay, man?" I blink a few times, clearing the unpleasant thoughts and glance to Prez. I don't know how long he was talking to me. If I think about those fucks, it's like it happened yesterday and sucks me back in.

"Yeah, Prez, I'm good. What's up?"

"I was tellin' y'all that ain't shit should be happening to me, but just in case. This is where the books and stuff is kept. All our dealin's—business-wise—and even the costs we spend on recreational shit. All that bull that went down with the Twisted Snakes not long ago got me thinkin' it would be easy for a big enough club to breach the compound. You two are the muscle of this club. I wanna rest easy knowin' you both know what needs protectin' if the five-oh or some rotten fucks show up. You feel me, son?"

"Gotcha. Ain't no worries, bro. You know we'll protect this club."

"I do know that. It's exactly why I wanted to include you both in this shit."

I look over at Cain, and he nods. I know he would die to protect his family, his club; so would I. Let's just hope it never comes to that.

We were dealing with some nasty shit when a club called the Twisted Snakes MC decided to start threatening the Prez's son, Brently. We eventually broke into their club, poisoned them all, and took them out to the pig farm not far from here. It got bloody, but the problem went away after that.

There's a knock on the office door, and we all pause, growing stiff because of the seriousness of the conversation. Cain and I step closer together to help hide the open floor behind us. No one should be around but club members, family, and the occasional club slut, but instinct has us doing our job of protecting.

I glance quickly at Prez and he nods, indicating for me to say something. Clearing my throat, I answer, "Yeah?"

She steps halfway into the doorway and glances at us, pausing briefly on me. Her lightly tanned skin calls to me, begging for me to caress it. She loves when I have my hands all over her...pulling, pinching, or spanking. I know she craves me just as much as I crave her.

"Umm, I was just checking to see if Prez had lunch or if he needs me to bring him something." Her voice causes my gut to tense. Her tone is silky smooth and feminine, the perfect combination to have any man hanging on to her every word.

Prez pops his head to the side of Cain's stocky legs so he can see her. "Thanks babe, but I'll be all right. I'll get something later."

"Are you sure? I can bring you something. I don't mind." She peers in at him innocently, and I swallow deeply as I take in her warm, honey colored eyes.

"Not now shug,' but I'll be out there later, I'm sure, wantin' some food."

She shoots him a friendly smile and nods. "Okay then." She briefly glances at us. "Boys," she acknowledges, nodding before she leaves the room. Releasing the breath I didn't realize I was holding, my stomach muscles finally relax.

"She's a sweet one, huh? Brother did good tyin' that one down." I nod at Prez but can't seem to make my mouth work. They all know I watch her. My brothers see how I look at her. Thank fuck no one talks about it, especially with the way these brothers around here like to gossip.

Cain reaches down and gives Prez his hand to help him up off the floor after he shuts the safe lid. "All right, I gotta head to the house to check on London and the kid. Little hellion almost caused her to shave off all of his hair the last time she cut it."

We all chuckle, remembering London's story of Jamison deciding to run after the dog right when she was trying to fade the sides of his hair. Then there's the time he thought the peanut butter was hair gel. He styled his little faux hawk with it, then smeared it over everything in the bathroom. That kid is something else; he's way too smart for his age.

Prez nods. "Give Momma some love, Cain. Take some of the stress off her, yeah?"

"Yeah, Prez, I got you."

He turns to me and fist bumps. "See ya, bro."

"Later."

"You want some grub, son?" Prez turns to me, blond eyebrow raised, after Cain is gone.

"No, thanks. I was gonna get a drink, unless you need me for sumthin'?"

"Nope. Shit's straight at the moment. You know I'll keep you informed."

"Yeah. How's Brently doing?"

He shrugs. "Just happy he's finally here, putting work in as a prospect. I'm happy to have my boy 'round the club where he belongs. Took him a long ass time to get here, but ain't gonna bitch now that he finally made it. How's he seem to you?"

"He doesn't talk much to me, that's why I was asking."

"Well, give it a little time, son. You're pretty cool with all the brothers. I'm sure he'll warm up. If not, he'll learn to, at least, respect ya'."

I grunt and follow Prez as we leave the office. He locks up, squeezing my shoulder as he pockets the key.

We head down the hall; he goes left toward the kitchen, and I veer toward the bar area over on the right. We're here at the clubhouse more than anyone else, so we're really comfortable with each other. We're both the loners. We both fucked up our relationships with our old ladies.

I can't believe I even had an ol' lady in the first place with how fucked up I am inside. Poor bitch never had a damn chance with me in a relationship. Well, not past the fuckin'. She was young and dumb. I wasn't emotionally available to her, but I was always faithful. I knew I didn't love her, but I never let her feel unwanted. Then the cunt had to

7

go whoring around to the MOBA, Mexican Outlaw Bikers Association, like those fucks even know what association means.

Walking behind the long bar, I snatch up a bottle of good whiskey and my usual tumbler. Lazy asses around here don't know how to wash shit, so I bought my own glass to use. I'm not going to drink after where some of their mouths have been.

I head to my usual booth. It's nice and worn. Pretty sure the cushion has my ass print permanently imbedded. It makes me look more normal size, like everyone else around here.

Placing the bottle and my tumbler on the table, I sit, slide to my spot, fill up my cup, and stretch my long legs out in front of me. I probably should have eaten with the Prez before I start drinking, but fuck it.

I take a few sips of the dark amber liquid, savoring the rich flavor as it goes down smoothly. It always makes the things I have to do a little easier. I can beat someone to death if needed, then have some whiskey to dull my thoughts of it all.

The club door opens wide and sunlight pours in, briefly blinding me from the brightness, as Shay struts in. She's this hot little Italian piece I've had some fun with. Doesn't hurt that she's a stripper and can give me some good private shows. Seeing the woman I want but can't fully have running around here, it's good to have a piece strutting around that I can fuck with if I want to.

Shay scans the room until her gaze lands on me, trudging over. "Hi, Ares." She plops down in the booth right next to me.

I'm going to have to talk to Scratch about letting chicks through the gate before calling me or Cain. Brother hasn't a fuckin' clue about security precautions. A set of tits doesn't mean they aren't dangerous. Brother sees a rack and pretty much goes dumb.

I grunt in response, not really in the mood for her today. I just watched the woman I want to be with enjoying herself with another man. I'm not jealous of her being happy. I just wish I was a piece of it.

"Are you grouchy?" Shay wraps her fingers around the hard muscle of my bicep and peers up at me with a slightly wrinkled forehead, concern written on her features. It's about time I start pulling away from this bitch. She's getting way too comfortable, latching onto me and shit. Pussy is good to have around, but I'm not trying to get another chick like my fuckin' ex.

"Nope." I shrug, glance at her quickly, and turn away.

I'm met with laughter, and it sends a tingle down my spine. I know that laugh. *They* walk through the bar. *She* has her arm laced through *his,* smiling happily. Of course, they're smiling. They're always fucking happy together.

"Brother!" He chortles, beaming a smile toward me, alongside hers.

"Yo."

"Goin' for a spin, you wanna come with?"

"No thanks, brother. Got some ass waiting," I grumble, and Shay giggles beside me, eating up the attention.

I shrug her off my arm, sit up, and take a long swallow of my whiskey. The gulp burns a little, but not much, being the seasoned drinker I am. I'm no alcoholic, but I've drunk my fair share.

"All right then, man. Have a good time."

I give him a two-finger salute, and he turns to leave. I briefly catch the glare *she* sends to Shay, her mouth stern and eyes shooting daggers, looking to kill.

I don't know why, but for some reason that little look makes me fucking stiff as a rod. My pants grow tight, and I shift my legs, thinking about taking her, about having them both right here in the bar, bending her over the bar top and eating her pussy while she sucks his cock.

They make their way outside, the club door slamming closed as they leave. A small hand caresses my leg, rubbing over my hard cock a few times and I growl, frustrated and fed up.

"You weren't kidding. You really are ready. You want it here or should we go to your room, daddy?" Shay questions excitedly.

"No, 'we' ain't headed nowhere, Shay. I wasn't talking about you and quit with the fuckin' daddy talk. I told you that shit ain't fuckin' cute."

"You're joking."

"Nope. Dead fuckin' serious."

She huffs. "Okay then, I guess this can happen another night."

Shay grabs her blue bag in a tiff, shouldering it and stands at the end of the table, hands on her hips, waiting. I glance up at her, eyebrow raised. "Well, should I come back in a few hours or make other plans?"

"Do what the fuck you want." I shrug, unconcerned.

"Fine, Ares. You have my number for when you're out of your bad mood." Shay spins, making her long dark brunette hair flail out in her wake.

Her gorgeous ass sways with her full hips as she heads back to the club door. She has a body made to taunt men, eliciting fantasies that will do nothing but get you in trouble. Too bad she doesn't fill my own fantasies. The door slams closed again as she stomps out. What is it with people always slammin' that fuckin' door?

I can't bring myself to care that she's upset. I know I should, but we first met by her dancing here. Shay was grinding all over my brothers and shit. I get it, that's her job and all, but any bitch I make mine won't be all up on every one of my brothers too. No one would have any respect for her after that shit.

Spin walks in from the back hall, heading straight for the bar. His ominous figure is decked out in jeans and a wife beater. He has his long black Mohawk in four big spikes up the center of his head, and his forehead is wrapped in a black bandanna. He has some sick ass tatts covering his arms.

He grabs a beer and swaggers toward me with a bored expression. Brother has some freaky ass eyes too. One of them is this weird violet-purple color and the other is grey. The guy has pussy swarming all over his tattoo shop wanting to be with him.

"You come in the back?" I question as he slides into the booth opposite me.

"Yep. Whatcha been up to?"

"Not a fucking thing. You?"

"Ain't shit. Shop was slow so I packed up early," he shrugs. "Wanna get inked?" He gestures with his chin to my knuckles. They always need touched up since I use them a lot. They're big and full of scars.

"Fuck yeah, let's do this."

"Bet."

"You know what? I feel like having a little party. You up for company?"

"Seriously, Ares? You know I'm down." He narrows his eyes at me. "I'm just surprised this is comin' from you." I nod and Spin pulls his phone out to start calling people up. I sit, nursing my whiskey, watching him send mass text messages to the brothers and God knows who else.

••••

I get a good buzz going on and before I know it, people are piling through the club door. Marilyn Manson's "Tainted Love" gets turned up and there is laughter and booze everywhere. A blonde and redhead grind with each other in the middle of the bar's floor, rubbing their hands all over each other's bodies, leisurely pulling clothing items off. The brothers eat it up, sitting so we can easily watch them.

Spin has a scantily clad little Asian on his lap, kissing all over his neck. His mouth is parted slightly, and his crazy colored eyes are glazed over in pleasure as he harshly grips each of her thighs in his hands.

Twist, my blond MC brother who's covered in traditional tattoos, does a few lines off the table near him, trying to relax. I doubt it'll help, probably wind him up even more. That brother has demons worse than my own, I think. He'll most likely end up getting into it with someone tonight. That's how he usually works, and normally it'll be 2

Piece or a prospect. There for a bit I thought Twist and 2 Piece were going to end up actually killing each other. Twist saved 2 Piece's life a while back from a few members out of a different club, and since then, things between them have calmed down.

I take a long pull off the Budweiser Scratch brought me, damn near draining half of the bottle. When I set the bottle down, Shay is in front of me. She smirks mischievously, dressed in a short black skirt and grey sequin halter top.

London cuts in before Shay has a chance to open her mouth. "Go get my man a beer," she orders, then turns and sits on Cain's lap as he sits between Twist and me. London's all dolled up in her pinup girl attire —red lips, big hair, cat eyes, and fitted old-fashioned skirt, looking the perfect part next to Cain. I think they are the sexiest fuckin' couple I've ever seen. 2 Piece and Avery are hot, but London and Cain could be on a fuckin' Harley magazine cover.

Shay glares, obviously peeved, but does as she's told. As far as bitches go around here, you don't fuck with London. Every brother respects London and her devotion to the club.

"Cupcake," Twist chortles, leaning over as London gives him a small kiss on the cheek.

"Twizzler." London smiles at him and then turns to me. "Hey, big man."

"Yo." I chin lift and fist bump Cain at the same time. I don't touch London. None of us do besides Twist. He treats her like a little sister, and Cain would go fuckin' nuts if another male got that close her, good friend or not. He's fiercely devoted to London and his kid, Jamison. I respect the fuck outta him for it too.

"How'z it, brother?"

"Good, man. I'm surprised so many people showed up." I throw my hand out, gesturing around the room.

"No shit, bro. No one ever hears 'Ares wants to party'. We all wanted to see what the fuck was goin' on." He chuckles and I grunt.

Shay hands London the beer for Cain and looks at me with her big puppy dog eyes. That shit doesn't work on me though. I ignore her as the club door opens, and I see 2 Piece and Avery walk in.

2 Piece scans the room, his eyes lighting up when they land on our little group. He tugs on Avery's hand, his weathered, tattooed skin clashing with her smooth and creamy complexion, leading her over to us. She looks happy to follow, her cheeks slightly flushed. She's wearing her signature daisy dukes with little lace shit around the bottom and a tank top. She has the best ass I've ever seen on a chick, both naked and with clothes on. Either she's warm from the Texas heat or he just got done fucking her, and I'm pretty goddamn jealous of that thought.

"Twist, Cain, Ares, 'sup?" 2 says as he pulls a seat up between me and Spin. Spin doesn't give a shit though; he's cool with 2 and fairly distracted by the Asian grinding on him.

I don't know if Avery really cares for Spin, though. Brother threatened to lock her ass in a closet when her Russian buddy Nikoli and 2 Piece were fighting over her awhile back. We all thought it was hilarious, but she was pretty fucking heated about it. Her man and her best friend going at each other's throats was enough for her to try to get people to jump in the middle. Spin schooled her real quick that around here we don't jump in on each other's shit unless it's absolutely necessary. The Oath Keepers MC is all about freedom and no judgment. If you can solve an issue with a few fists meeting flesh, then so fuckin' be it. Just one of the many things I love about the club.

Avery leans down, hugging London. They kiss each other on the lips, and I know the Brothers can't help but imagine what it would look like with the two of them together. Fuck! That shit would be off-the-chain hot.

Avery stands, then turns to me, her sweet scent hitting me full force with her movement. She grazes her soft petite palm on my cheek, rubbing my scruffy dark beard; I tilt my head and lean into it slightly.

She bends toward me, giving me a short, tender kiss on my lips. I swallow harshly when her lips meet mine, as feelings explode through my body, attempting to pull me under. My hands turn to fists as I clench my fingers tightly together to keep myself from pulling her to me.

After a bittersweet moment, she pulls back. Her lustful eyes are full of heat as she stares into mine, then she shifts her warm honey irises toward 2 Piece. Avery shoots me a small smile, resting her hands on my large shoulders as she leans back up. With one small squeeze to my shoulder, she releases me to sit on 2 Piece's lap.

I glance at him quickly to meet his gaze as he smirks knowingly. He knows exactly what she fucking does to men, and he loves it. His smirk makes me feel fucking stupid and I grit my teeth, trying to tamper down the beast inside, taunting me with memories.

●●●●

My mother used to smirk at me a lot. Every time she would fuck someone in front of me, she'd have the same cocky little smirk painted on her worn face. A few specific memories stand out, always in the shadows, waiting to haunt me.

I remember her placed in the middle of the thin old blue rug. My mother's stringy black hair, frizzy and halfway torn out from her ponytail. Her black and blue knees on the floor spread apart, looking small and boney. The fat man who had just been fucking her earlier, holding his thick black leather belt wrapped tightly around her throat as he stood behind her, pulling it tighter and tighter through the bronze clasp.

He chuckled gleefully, his voice full of evil as she was unable to speak anymore, her face going from deep red to a bluish and then finally fading to an odd pale color. My mother's disgusting fake moans I was always forced to hear, finally cut off. I can still see her wide, empty brown eyes staring at me, almost pleading for me to do something. I sat in the corner, smirking, while I watched the life being drained from her.

I can't remember how old I was; life was very scary and confusing back then. I know she fucked a bunch of random men to make money, and she always ended up giving the money she received to my father. Not that my father was around much, and when he was, he was even harsher on me than she was. Fucking prick.

••••

"You want another beer, Ares? Or how about I dance for you?" Shay pulls me from my last memory of my mother in the living room, by running her hand along my arm.

All these fucking couples around, and I sit here alone. Shay doesn't count. She'll jump all over someone else's dick in a heartbeat. It's probably for the best I'm alone, since I'm pretty fucked up. I wish I was a better man, but I enjoy being sinister a little too much. It helps me feed the demon lurking inside.

"Dance," I grunt as "Cowboy" by Kid Rock plays loudly and she smiles, seeming pleased I'm giving her my attention. Shay loves any attention she can get from men.

Her hips sway side to side with the beat, her skirt edging up slightly, just enough so that I can see the little crease at the bottom of her ass cheeks. My brothers and me all sit back and watch her. There's one thing Shay can do well and that's dance. Her sinful thighs part, giving sneak peeks of a purple scrap of material, barely covering her pussy.

She turns, facing me, rubbing her hands over her tits. Her bra straps fall off her shoulders and she sucks on her plump bottom lip.

I'm surprised when I feel a soft, petite hand in mine and fingers wind through my own. Clearing my throat, I glance over at Avery and she grins, her eyes alight with mischief. Reminds me of the very first time I met her. No one in the club really knew about her. 2 Piece had been sneaking her in his room so none of us had met her yet.

••••

I was standing in the hallway next to the bar, chugging whiskey. There's a little closet, used to store kegs, with missing doors that I like to drink next to sometimes. I don't normally down liquor like that, but I was trying to chase away the fucking memories I battle with.

A door down the hall opens and "La Grange" by ZZ Top pours out of the room until the door shuts, silencing the hallway again. I turn away but I'm taken off guard when a hot little thing with Auburn hair and a nice thick, round booty walks past me.

My right arm darts out, snatching her before she gets too far away from me, and I slam her small body into the kegs as my large, rough hand rests around her throat.

"Who are you?" I growl so deeply you'd think I was fucking Batman or something.

"I'm Avery," she squeaks, the pulse in her throat fluttering like a scared butterfly under my fingers.

"Oh yeah? Is it my turn now, Avery?"

"I'm seeing 2 Piece."

"I get it. You a new club slut?" Relaxing my grip slightly so I don't crush the new toy, I lean in smelling her pretty brownish hair. It makes me think of fall with the red running through it. She's really well-manicured compared to the normal club whores around here.

I drop the whiskey bottle to the floor, running my now free hand over her right breast, across her ribs, and straight down into her tiny shorts.

I gaze at Avery sitting beside me now, as I remember staring into her wild eyes that night, how she looked as I thrusted my thick fingers into her hot, wet core.

They widen as I go in deep, my cock growing so fucking hard as she clamps down around my fingers, her body asking me to give it more.

I squeeze her dainty throat a little, loving the fact I can easily take her life; that I hold all of the power right in my hand. Her small fingers

16

grasp onto my arm strongly, bright pink and purple nails digging deeply into my skin, as I pump in and out of her tightness a few times. The shit I could do to this bitch. She's so fucking responsive, I could make her melt in no time.

When she tries to speak I loosen my hand, her stuttering out, "No-no I'm not a whore, and I'm on-only seeing 2 Piece."

I drop my hand from her neck, pulling my fingers free as I back away from her. For fuck's sake, she *could* be my brother's girl, and I had no idea.

She stands still, her chest rising and falling rapidly as she huffs out a few breaths. I lightly flick over her erect nipple with the pad of my thumb, making her already rosy colored cheeks deepen further. I can't help it; she has on nothing but a goddamn plain white T-shirt and some small shorts with lace around the bottom. She might as well have stepped off of the biker calendar hanging in the Prez's office.

"Sorry 'bout that, angel." Muttering, I gesture to the bar with my chin and she lets out a whoosh of air, turning to continue her trek to the bar on shaky legs. Guilt washes over me as I stare at her ass while she walks away.

Guilt, because even her being my brother's chick, I still want her something fierce. Even after finding *that* out, I *still* had to touch her nipple. I wanted to slip it in my mouth so fuckin' bad and bite it; I wanted to make her fucking scream for me.

Shaking my head, I walk to my own room, unsatisfied and angry, and slam the door. I can still remember that first taste I had of her on my tongue, when I had placed my fingers in my mouth. She was long gone when I had gotten to my room, but I savored her sweet flavor.

••••

My lustful daze fades when Shay makes herself comfortable by plopping down on my lap, and Avery drops my hand like she was burned. No doubt Shay feels my erection; I'm hard from that memory of my run-in with Avery. Knowing Shay, she probably thinks it's from watching her dance, but that couldn't be further from the truth. Avery owns every hard inch of it.

Shay leans in and wraps her arms around my neck, pushing her breasts close to my face.

"The fuck, Shay?" I grumble, pulling my head back away from her cleavage.

"I feel it, baby...so glad you liked that dance." She wiggles, rotating her hips so her ass puts pressure on my dick.

"I told you nothing was happening tonight. I don't know how to be any clearer."

She glares and stands up angrily. "What the fuck are you going to do with your cock then? You already have a new bitch somewhere around here?" She looks around the room. "I don't see her right now." Shay's voice draws the attention of everyone and eyes shoot to us. I think the entire room hears me growl.

I stand swiftly, my metal chair flinging out behind me as I bellow, "Scratch! Come get this bitch now!" Her body slides off of mine and she clutches my hand strongly in both of hers.

"No, baby. That's not necessary," Shay pleads. I step to the side, yanking my hand out of hers.

"You know the fucking rules, Shay." Pointing in her face, I drive my point in. "Go home."

"Ares, don't do this."

I gesture to Scratch and he comes scampering over quickly. "Get her the fuck out," I say. "No more bitches without approval."

"Okay, sorry about that, Ares."

Nodding, I turn, fixing my chair to sit back down.

"Fuck it. I'm out," I grumble loudly, to no one in general.

Instead of sitting, I head straight to my room. I don't have time to deal with any fuckin' drama. I'm too drunk at this point and I don't trust myself to not start up any shit with anyone.

ARES

two days later

PREZ TURNS TO ME AS EVERYONE LEAVES AFTER OUR WEEK-ly church meeting. "Just a sec, Ares." He orders and takes a drink of his bottled water. I think he and Cain are the only two in the whole club that regularly drink bottled water, bunch of damn health junkies.

I nod, watching the brothers finish filing out of the chapel.

Eventually the door closes and Prez begins, "I need to talk to you 'bout some issues I'm dealing with. No one 'round here knows about 'em, and I wanna keep it like that."

"You know whatever you say will be kept between us, Prez."

"Good," he steeples his fingers, gazing at me with his blue eyes surrounded by a few weathered wrinkles. After several moments, he practically breathes out the words, low and troubled. "Mona has cancer."

"The fuck?" I burst, taken off guard.

Not everyone knows about the Prez and his family life. Mona was his Old Lady before some shit popped off with Smile's. I don't know exactly what happened, but I know something did and she eventually left the Prez. Mona took his kids, with him willingly giving up everything. I've been around the Prez long enough that I know Mona, his son Brently, and his daughter Princess.

He's stressed and winces as he runs his hands through his long blond hair. "I know, it fuckin' surprised me too. Mona didn't tell me much about it. I just know it's getting bad. Brently is clueless and Princess won't even fuckin' talk to me."

"Shit, Prez, if I can do anything," I trail off, having no clue what help I could possibly offer him or any of them. I didn't have a real family who would have cared about this shit, and I don't have a wife, but I truthfully have no idea what he's going through.

Prez nods, his forehead wrinkled slightly and eyes strained, full of worry. "Thanks, son. I 'preciate it. I'm gonna have a vote. You been doin' the VP's job without the patch. I think it's time you get that patch you deserve. Not only that, but I'm gonna be missin' a lot, and I can trust you to take care of this club like I try to. I need to go and help take care of Mona as much as I can. I know she will fight me at every turn, stubborn ass woman, but I will never forgive myself if I don't at least try. I gave up on her so easily before; I have to step in now."

"Prez, I'm not no vice president," I argue, shaking my head. "I'm honored you would think that of me, but I can't do that job."

"Son, listen to me. You already do that job. Hell, when you boys was in Tennessee, you did my fuckin' job too. I know that if I'm not around or if something happens to me, you know what to do. You're more devoted to this club than anyone I know, and the brothers look up to you. They don't just give that kind of respect to anyone, Ares."

"If you really believe that, then I'll do it. I don't know if I'll do the patch justice, but I'll damn sure do my fuckin' best."

"Good. I'm going to put up a vote for Cain to be moved into Enforcer also. Whatcha think about it?"

"I think he's done the work and deserves the patch. He'll be a good fit, and the brothers will pass it with no issues."

"Good, then we'll make it happen. Next week at church, we'll put up the votes and see what the brothers have to say."

I nod, taking a swallow from my now lukewarm beer.

"I'm also gonna tell the girls to get a big BBQ planned for next Wednesday, 'cause I know everyone will want to celebrate. Yesterday's turned out great, and we need more functions like that 'round here. Those women can cook!" He finishes with a small grin, but I still can't shake the feeling that I won't be strong enough to wear that patch.

"Prez, what if the brothers don't vote on it like you think?"

Sighing, he gestures toward the chair beside him. "Relax, Ares. Everyone knows you belong in this seat next to me. Besides that, if anything were to ever happen, you deserve this spot I sit in—not anyone else. *You.*"

"All right then," I grunt, staring at the seat placed between him and me. We haven't had a VP in a very long time.

Prez stands, running his tattoo-covered fingers down his plain shirt, straightening himself. I guess old habits don't go away, even as a biker. He pats my shoulder as he passes me on his way to the door. The bar noise trickles inside the silent room as he escapes out into the loud room, overflowing with members.

I sit and stare a few moments more at the chair I'll soon be expected to fill. It's old and the leather is broken in and slightly faded in the wooden frame, but it's the closest to the head of the table, and that's all that really matters. Fuck, I never once expected for this to be happening. I'm honored he would choose me and that he feels that the brothers will accept me into the VP spot so easily. Being the Enforcer, I guess it would be an option for him to think of me for that spot, but there are many other patched members who would be happy with the spot also.

I hope this doesn't cause any kind of beef with Smiles. That brother has been in the club longer than me and probably should be the one up for the vote instead. With his and Prez's shit going on, I don't think he will ever switch from his spot though. I hope the doctors and Prez are able to help Mona out. Cancer fuckin' sucks.

I eventually move from my seat, glancing around our church room that is even more significant to me now, as I head out toward the bar. I want to be the one to tell Cain the good news, but I have to keep this shit locked up tight till it actually happens. I've always been the one Prez confides in, but shit like this makes me want to share it with my boy, Cain.

Scratch notices me approaching. He hurries to get my personal glass ready, pulling a full bottle of whiskey from the shelf and sets it all on the bar top for me.

"Thanks, but I just want a Coke," I say, shrugging as I scoot the bar stool over.

"A Coke? Ares?" Scratch peers at me like I'm delusional and he's never heard me ask for a Coke before.

"Yep, 'bout time I start keeping my head clear durin' the day. I ain't no fuckin' alcoholic or anything. Give me a Coke, Scratch."

"No problem." He nods, putting the whiskey bottle back on the shelf, filling up my cup with Coke from the soda gun. He eyes me during the entire process, curious.

Little fucker is probably wondering if this is some sort of a test. I don't miss being a prospect for anything. That shit blew—always wondering if everything you did was being watched and if somethin' stupid would stop you from getting voted on. I should find out how the boys came across Scratch in the first place, especially if I'm going to be the VP. It's my job to protect the club, but now it'll be my job to be informed on everything also.

As soon as my glass of soda hits the bar top, I snatch up my cup. "Thanks, Prospect. Next time don't move so fuckin' slow."

He nods and scurries away to the other end of the bar.

Good. I should intimidate him right now. I haven't had the chance to break him in properly yet. Maybe I'll have Cain do it, so I can make sure he's familiar with all his shit as an Enforcer. We'll make Scratch's skinny ass into a man eventually.

Turning, I scan the bar and come across my brothers crowded

around a few tables, laughing and bullshitting with each other. We always have a drink and relax after church if there aren't any pressing matters to tend to. The club life is all about being free and happy.

Avery and 2 Piece are sitting comfortably at my usual booth, so I make my way over to them, sitting across from the love birds.

2 Piece puts his fist out and I pound it. "Yo, 'sup, brother?" I nod briefly at Avery and then turn back to 2.

"Hey, man. Everything straight with Prez?"

Avery's eyes grow wide. She's so fucking nosey, but it makes her even more adorable. She's always curious about anything she can find out that has to do with the club. She's more curious than a kitten.

"Yeah, he's straight." I shrug and leave it at that.

It's clearly none of his business what I talk to the Prez about. Once 2 Piece steps up at the table wanting more responsibilities, then he will be let in on more of what's left out of church discussions. He likes his freedom and we respect that, giving him the space and independence he craves.

2 Piece nods and Avery shifts, scooting into the booth next to me, bringing her damn pup along with her. I love this little Doberman, Lily, but the ass has chewed up so much of my shit. Whenever 2 Piece and Avery take off on a ride, I take care of Lily for them. The last time, the fucking dog shit on my belt. I couldn't get pissed though, because she's just a pup. I damn sure let 2 Piece have it when I called his ass though. Brother brought me home a ton of beef jerky, trying to make up for it, so it ended up working out.

Avery sits up on her knees, places the puppy next to her, and lands a whisper soft kiss on my cheek.

My dick pulses with the tender touch. Avery and I both like kinkier shit, and I swear the bitch owns a piece of my heart even if she belongs to 2 Piece. I can't help it though. Ever since that first night I stopped her in the hallway, she's slowly weaseled her way in. Now she's in the club all the time and always doin' sweet shit like giving me kisses. It really fucks with my feelings for her. I keep holding myself back, but it seems to get harder and harder every single day.

I could seriously use a distraction around here, but Shay had to go. Too bad that bitch I met on the run we did to Tennessee, Lindsay, don't live closer. Lindsay and her friend Sarah could fuck for hours, bunch of crazy chicks. I thought Sarah was gonna rip Cain's clothes off when she saw him in the hotel room that day. Cain was all types of fucked up over shit goin' down with London though, so I had kicked the girls out of the motel room. Poor dude was a huge mess until he got London back home and in his bed permanently.

"Did you hear me?" 2 Piece questions and I take a large gulp of my Coke, clearing the memories away from that crazy trip we all took together. 2 Piece first met Avery on that run, but I wasn't that lucky.

"Nah," I shake my head, finally giving him my attention. "What was that?"

"I asked if you were up to havin' a little fun tonight? Avery has been all over my nuts 'bout having you with us again. She fuckin' aches for you, I know it."

"Come on, Silas," Avery whispers, interrupting him. "You know that you enjoy it too."

"Yeah, free bird, I do enjoy it. I know it makes you feel good. I'm all for you being satisfied, Shorty. I wanna keep my girl as happy as possible."

Her head darts back toward me with a wide, white smile and a twinkle in her eye. "So, do you want some, Ares?" She murmurs huskily.

Her voice melts over my insides and I swear to Christ I would take her in this booth in front of every single member in the club if she would let me. I know that won't happen, but it's fine. I'll take her any way I can have her, at any time she's willing. "Fuck!" I grumble, burning up inside for her already. "Avery, you know I always want that dirty little mouth, or round ass, whatever you feel like givin,' angel."

2 Piece chuckles, watching us with a smile. The fucker knows Avery is absolutely gorgeous and a great fuck. Hell, they are both fucking

amazing, in and out of the bed. I wish he would let me have him too. I don't know if we will ever be at that stage together. It takes everything in me to hold back from him and not take him like I really want to, especially when I catch him watching me with Avery. I could make him feel so good, he just doesn't realize it.

"Fuck it, let's go," I grunt and stand.

2 Piece scoops the pup and Lily up and they follow my lead as I head to their room. The brothers all watch us go. They know what's goin' on, but they better not say a damn word about it to Avery. She's a good girl, real sweet and don't need no body making her feel judged. The brothers have all seen me fuck many chicks and know I don't give a shit, but Avery don't like any sort of attention about us having threesomes. I think she's afraid the brothers won't respect her anymore; she doesn't realize the crazy bastards are just jealous and want to watch.

I shuffle over to the side of the door and out of the way. 2 enters the room first, placing Lily in her kennel with her favorite small fleece blanket. Avery trails in behind him, stepping into the room.

She gets one step through the doorway before I reach out, grabbing a large handful of hair. I wrench her head back and she yelps as the back of her body collides with the solid front of mine.

I'm positive she can feel me hard in my pants. I'm aching to feel her tightness wrapped around my cock. Fuck, I've been so hard since we were at the booth, it's a fuckin' miracle I didn't poke anyone on the way through the bar.

Tilting her head to the side, I lick up the side of her smooth, delicate neck. Her body shudders in delight, and her nipples stiffen through her little pink spaghetti strap shirt. It's so fucking sexy to see her hard peeks, begging for attention.

"Do you want some, angel?" I murmur next to the soft shell of her ear, repeating her question from earlier when she made me feel like I could burst in my pants.

"Fuck, yes!" she gasps out, her voice glazed over with lustful need.

Wonton thoughts are most likely dancing in her head at this point, ready and willing to bend to my will.

2 Piece gazes at us, grinning, amused. His pants are tight as well, the outline of his cock telling me he enjoys what he sees.

He turns up his radio a little and starts stripping his clothes off. His black T-shirt flies across the room into a heap, per his usual. The faded blue jeans slide smoothly down his tattooed, muscular thighs until he's left in only a pair of fitted white boxer briefs. His colorful tattooed sleeves and thighs stand out in contrast to the simple plain material. He's absolutely fucking delectable. God, I wish I could taste him.

He grins as I peer at him, my mouth salivating at each curve and indention of muscle adorning his body, while biting and sucking on Avery's neck. I release her hair, running my hands over her tummy until I reach her small breasts, tweaking her gorgeous peeks with each of my hands.

Her body trembles with need under my touch as 2 Piece slides the last bit of material completely off. His cock stands at attention, swollen and ready to join in on some fun. I bet he would love having my large hands wrapped firmly around his dick, pumping him until he begs me to let him finish. I wouldn't let him finish though. I'd play with him until his bones locked tight and he shook with intense pleasure.

2 Piece approaches, easily flicking Avery's pants button loose and pulling her fitted jeans down her lightly tanned legs. With one last little pinch on her nipples, I take a step back.

I attempt to concentrate on taking my own clothes off. The basic white T-shirt gets placed on the little chair off to the side. My pants come down, exposing my full cock, and I slip my black jeans off as I slide my feet free from my black leather boots. My pants land somewhere as I'm drawn in, watching the stunning couple together. I always try to be tidy, I know 2 is sort of a neat freak, but I can't help myself as I witness the love and affection that radiates between them.

2 Piece softly caresses Avery's stomach, his tattooed hands dwarf-ing her small stomach underneath them, while sweetly kissing over

her breasts.

She clutches onto his shoulders as if she's holding on for dear life, never wanting to let go of him. "I love you, Silas," she lovingly croons, staring at him with adoration. I can't help the painful shot of emptiness hitting my gut like a knife, twisting as deeply as possible. I've never had this feeling so strongly before.

It was always there while watching them, but never to this degree. This` time it feels as if my soul is being fed into a meat grinder over and over. Biting the inside of my cheek roughly enough to get a small rush of copper flavor to flood my taste buds, I wrench the feelings away. This is about her, about pleasing both of them. This has nothing to do with me. I need to control myself, put my needs on the back burner, and just accept that this is the only way I can have them. I have to cherish 2 Piece and Avery in these times. I never know when it may be the last time I witness them so vulnerable with me included.

I clear my throat, alerting them that I'm indeed ready to be a part of the action. 2 Piece knows I struggle when I'm not the one being fully in control. I had all control stripped from me when I was younger, so now it practically consumes me.

I always fight with myself inside and attempt to back off some with these two. Avery is still somewhat new to everything I like, and I don't want to overpower 2 Piece sometime, making things awkward between us. I'm honored he trusts me enough to share these experiences together, but make no mistake, if he ever allows me to unleash, it would be a completely different experience for both of them

Avery backs up a few steps so I can feel her warmth against my body. The little minx reaches behind her back, grabbing onto my dick roughly and giving it a hefty squeeze. "Mmmph."

I groan, clenching my teeth together. I grab a handful of her hair again and walk her forward enough to finally kick the door shut as I go. I'm sure if any of the brothers walked down the hallway, they fully enjoyed the sight.

We stop right before the bed and I release her silky hair, running my hands down her sun-kissed shoulders, she glances back at me as I grip the top of her shirt in both hands. I peer into her eyes, heatedly, my need smoldering for her as I rip the thin material in half, down her back. Her chest rises with each excited, turned-on breath, and 2 Piece grabs her chin, turning her back to face him.

Wrapping the small straps between my thick fingers, I easily snap each of the dainty strings over her shoulders that hold the shirt up. The thin pink material cascades to the floor, and 2 takes her mouth, owning it with a strong kiss. Not one to be left out, I bend down slightly, reaching for the material while licking up her spine. I hear her muffled moan and it lets me know she hasn't completely forgotten me back here.

She breaks the kiss with 2 Piece, panting. "Oh, yes!"

Turning her face slightly toward her shoulder, I wrap the material over her eyes, creating a makeshift blindfold, securely tying the material in the back. Now 2 Piece and I get to take in her beautiful nakedness without her knowing what exactly we're looking at or planning to touch. It's almost like a game. I know her mind is racing trying to guess what will happen. At the same time, it's almost hard to decide what to do first, all of the delectable possibilities on display right in front of us.

Now, it's finally my turn to take her mouth. After watching the kiss between them, it feels as if I've been waiting forever to graze my lips against hers. My mouth meets hers fervently, and I can still taste 2 on her tongue. The flavors exploding through me gets me so wound up, it makes my dick feel like it's going to burst. I experience not only kissing her, but I also get to imagine what it would be like thrusting my powerful tongue inside *his* warm, wet mouth. Would he let me control the kiss or would he fight me for it? Would he follow my lead, maybe grip onto my chest tightly, while I showed him he wasn't only meant for a woman?

2 Piece's hand brushes against mine, delicately stroking Avery's collar bone, eliciting goose bumps on her skin and drawing me away

from the passionate kiss. I get utterly lost in her every time I get to sample her sweet lips. Pulling back, I meet his gaze and he nods, gesturing toward the bed.

Bending to accommodate Avery's short height, I scoop her up, bridal style, in my arms. I'm so large compared to her; she's like a feather. I love how she feels as her hands grasp onto my shoulder and neck to hold on. She holds on leisurely, like she's confident that I won't let her fall. She's right, though. I would never let harm come to her.

Avery giggles as I move with her and it calms my thoughts, that empty feeling rotting out the inside of my stomach melts away and is dusted with her warmth once again. To know I bring her any type of joy is worth the restrictive control I have to show, suppressing my true feelings for them. Each time I feel her, every time I see him vulnerable, I get a little deeper in with the both of them. I'm probably too much of a bastard to have a heart worth filling, but they make me want it full.

I quickly shoot 2 a grin, then toss her easily on the bed. Avery bounces slightly on her side, squealing in surprise. He chuckles at me, playing with her while prowling toward her, like she's his last meal.

Experiencing his body in these angles like this have me gripping my dick savagely. Fuck, he's amazing. The back muscles on him alone are enough to make me want to smack his ass a few good times.

"Turn her, brother, and get those panties off," I order gruffly, swallowing down the need to tell him to lie beside her so I can have them both the way I really want them—eating her out like it's my fucking dying wish, alongside of fucking him crazily.

2 Piece listens, pulling her pink thong down her thighs with his teeth. He tosses the underwear at me and I catch them, bringing the exquisite material to my nose before tossing them over with my pants. Avery smells so goddamn delicious. I need to taste that sweet cunt of hers.

"It's been awhile, Ares. What do you want first?"

I lick my lips, staring at his mouth. If he only knew I wanted him on his knees, with my cock shoved halfway down his throat, he wouldn't be asking.

"I wanna eat her cunt, you?"

Avery squirms, rubbing her legs together. "I'm completely okay with that idea," she interrupts and I silently chuckle.

"Aww, shorty, you bein' cute, huh?" 2 Piece cocks his eyebrow at her, then turns to me. "Maybe we should spank her?"

"Get four belts," I tell him.

"I don't have four belts, man."

I strip my belt out of my pants and then go to his jeans, doing the same. Walking back to the bed, I notice her mouth parted, she has quick little bursts of air coming out.

I know she heard me jingle the belts when I was undoing our wallet chains next to them. Her mind has to be racing inside, wondering what we're going to do with the belts. I wonder if she thinks I'm gonna hit her with them. I might pop her lightly with one sometime if we reach that level, but she's not ready for that yet.

Shrugging, I hold up the belts that I was able to collect. "It's all good. We'll make these two work."

"Umm, what exactly are you doing with the belts?" She stutters out, her voice edgy.

2's head turns toward her swiftly as he chastises her. "Shorty, you know I want you quiet when we're in here."

Avery takes a deep breath, drawing in a little dose of courage. That's just one of the many reasons why I want her so badly. She's always so fucking brave, no matter what it is. She faces shit when she needs to and doesn't back out. She's a little fighter inside, just like I've always been.

Tossing 2 Piece a belt, I nod at his side so he'll know where to attach it. We tie each of her ankles to the metal footboard. Avery made him get a fancy iron bed, and it's 'bout time we put it to its real use. I should have already had her fine ass tied to it. I'll remedy that and initiate things sooner next time if needed.

"Hold her hands. I don't want any interruptions," I bark.

2 Piece moves to the top of the bed, sitting on the pillows and holds her wrists together above her head. His cock bobs, ready to play.

Her pussy lips glisten as they're spread before me like it's a fucking Thanksgiving dinner, and I finally get to have some dessert. I climb on the bed over one of her legs, until I'm resting between her thighs, right where I want to be.

"That's some pretty pink you have here, angel," I grumble against her swollen lips. I stick my tongue in her center and she flexes with need, squeezing it to get more.

"*Ohhhh!*" Avery cries out.

2 Piece muffles her, using one hand to cover her mouth. He likes to shut her up, makes her get all turned on and even louder. I go to town and nibble on her clit a few times, applying more pressure on it with my tongue.

"Brother," 2 Piece grunts heavily, turned on, after a few moments of watching me.

"Hmm?" I start to suck ruthlessly as her legs bend and dart to the sides, squirming.

"I want in her. I can't wait. It's too fuckin' hot, seeing you making her feel so fuckin' good."

I sit back, resting on my knees, reaching over and dutifully untying each of her ankles. I rub each foot briefly, relieving the skin from the indentions caused by her pulling against the belts.

Once she's free from my grip, 2 lies beside Avery and I help direct her body to climb on top of him. He opens the condom he had resting on the pillow next to him and quickly slides it on between them. 2 rubs the head of his dick against her wetness and then easily glides her onto his hard shaft.

I use the brief break to slide on my own Magnum I had gotten from my wallet when I had retrieved the belts.

Avery straddles him, his knees bent up and spread, making her completely exposed from behind. I see clearly his dick seated inside her core, her pussy creaming with wetness around it, his sac lying heavily and a peek of his own tight hole. My dick rejoices inside, hardening further at the amazing sights right in front of me.

I lie down between his spread knees, savoring the absolutely amazing sight before me. Starting with Avery, I lick up all of her juices, occasionally swiping the bottom of his shaft with my tongue. She starts to move slightly, so 2 Piece begins rocking her leisurely, since he's distracted with her, I lick his sac, witnessing them tighten up for a moment, he probably thinks I grazed them on accident.

Rather than stop, I pull them into my mouth, drawing on each one deeply.

"Oh fu-ck," he moans.

I can't wait any longer. I lick up to Avery's anus, using some of her own juices for lubrication. I'm fucking kinky, so this shit turns me on even more than if I was just to lick her plain or use lube. To know she's surrounding me, even her wetness, is beyond erotic.

I sit back up on my knees, aligning my hefty cock up to her entrance, and begin working myself gradually and tenderly into her. The sensations are fucking insane. I can feel my dick rubbing against 2's cock inside of her. I curl my toes, gritting my teeth. It feels so good it's almost maddening.

2 Piece and I trade off, entering her and pulling out, always in an even rhythm. We're in sync with each other in more ways than one...if only he would start to notice it.

"Goddamn, you feel fuckin' phenomenal, angel."

"Yes," Avery moans and my dick throbs, as her sexy raspy voice magnetizes the sensations floating throughout my body.

I suck on two of my fingers, priming them for 2 Piece. He didn't protest my little mouth exploration I did earlier, so I'm going to push him a little further.

I place the opposite hand on the bed, bracing myself just in case this doesn't go over well. I reach between my legs with my other hand. He grunts as I brush his nuts, finding my way to his hole. The next drive I make deeply into Avery, I thrust my fingers into him at the same time.

"Fuuuck, fuck, fuck!" He gasps. I'm met with some resistance as I pump my fingers into him twice. His dick starts to throb crazily, losing control and erupting inside Avery.

I pull my hand free, using it to grip her hip, as he starts rubbing circles on her clit, biting her neck where she likes it, making her shoot off next. His eyes are closed, so I have no clue how to read what he's feeling, and it makes me a little nervous inside.

"Ohhhhhh!" Avery screams, freezing up as she rides through her intense orgasm and I clamp my hand over her mouth, effectively muffling her. It's amazing if nobody thinks we're in here fuckin' killin' her.

She collapses in an exhausted heap on top of 2 as I continue to move inside her tight hole. I watch 2 Piece over her shoulder and finally after a few beats he meets my gaze. He knows what just happened, and he knows he fucking loved it.

2 Piece doesn't say anything, just watches me, never breaking eye contact as I pump into Avery a few more times, eventually emptying myself into the condom, experiencing one of the most gratifying orgasms I've had in quite a long time. It just happened, but all I can think of is doing it again. I want to watch his eyes this time as I thrust my fingers in him, making him cry out. I know it won't happen though. It's too soon.

The spell is broken when Lily starts to whine in her cage. She's not used to being locked up in her kennel when people are in here. Eventually with the right training, she won't have to be locked up at all. Poor girl, it's probably her dinnertime, and she's tired of waiting.

Pressing a tender kiss to Avery's shoulder, I rise carefully, climbing over their depleted bodies and heading into the small bathroom. I take care of the condom, flushing it and wash my hands with the girly smelling soap on the counter.

Avery and 2 Piece are lying comfortably in the middle of the bed snuggling when I finish with the restroom.

She sends me a tired, sated smile. "Ares, come lie down and relax with us." Avery gestures with her hand for me to come closer.

Grinning slightly, I shake my head. "Nah, angel, not really my style. How about I take Lily outside and get her dinner? You can stay in bed and rest up."

"That sounds wonderful, Ares. Thank you so much."

I nod, glancing briefly at 2 Piece. He watches me the entire time, wearing a contemplative look. I know he must be questioning everything that just happened. I'll find out soon if we're going to have more fun or if he will pull away completely. It will fuckin' hurt losing him, but I can only control myself so much when it comes to being with them both like this.

Pulling on my dark jeans, I tuck my shirt into the back of my pants so it hangs out like a shop towel. I slide my feet into my boots, grabbing Lily's dog food. She has her own bowl in my room also, so I just need her and the food.

"You're good?" I question Avery, peering over her worriedly. I don't think I hurt her in any way, but I still want to make sure. I was hurt too much growing up. I would never want to hurt anyone I care about in any way, ever.

"Yes, we're great, Ares." She beams a bright smile, and I grin even bigger at her. She's so fuckin' beautiful.

"Cool, then we're out. Later." I grab Lily's kennel, stuffing the dog food under the same arm and leave their room. The good-bye part is definitely always the weirdest.

ARES

one week later

MY CHEST PUFFS OUT WITH PRIDE AS I LEAVE THE CHAPEL. The vote happened, and it all passed. I'm the new vice president of the Oath Keepers MC.

Cain got his vote and patch showing he's the new club Enforcer. The vote then moved to 2 Piece also, even though he wasn't in church today. The brothers voted him on as the new Sergeant-at-Arms. He was already pretty much handling any kind of weapons deals we've had and working alongside the Road Captain, Smiles, coordinating the runs to transport our weapons business we have going. He's done a great job so far and deserves the recognition.

Prez said he'd call him in the office later to discuss it with 2 Piece and make sure he's good with it, but as far as everyone's concerned he already has the spot. I couldn't be more pleased with how everything turned out today. I'm a little surprised it went over so smoothly, but I'm not gonna complain one bit.

I head outside to get in a quick smoke. Sometimes when I get excited or deal with getting rid of a really bloody body, I'll have a smoke. I don't do it nearly as much as I used to or Cain will bitch at me about my health like he has a damn vagina between his legs.

The back door of the club closes behind me and I walk straight into 2 Piece going to town on Sadie. He's yelling at her about seeing Twist again. Being her big brother, it's eating him up inside that she and Twist have been getting really cozy lately.

Sadie takes off past me in a rush, heading inside the club, appearing a little embarrassed that I caught the tail end of their conversation.

"Calm the fuck down, brother." I place my hands on 2 Piece's chest, trying to get him to take a few breaths. He knows Twist wants his little sister, and it's been driving him nuts all week. I don't know what exactly happened this week to set him off more, but he's been like a goddamn bear toward people and a few are starting to get sick of it.

"Fuck that, man. My sister is already pregnant by God knows who. Twist needs to stop sniffin' around Sadie. He's no good for her, we all know it. She's had enough shit to deal with, she don't need to be dealin' with fuckin' Twist of all people."

"Look, I get that it's your sister, but you gotta let her make her own decisions. Ever since you guys came back from Cali, he's been taking care of her and that babe."

"I don't give a mother fuck. *I* take care of her."

"Yo, it can't be like that anymore. You have Avery. She needs to be taken care of first. You might not wanna hear this shit, but Sadie is a fuckin' grown ass woman. Back off some, brother."

"Are you fucking kidding?" He barks, looking like he's ready to head-butt me.

As soon as Cain steps through the club door out back, he's beside me, probably from hearing all of the yelling. We must be getting loud if people are hearing it inside. "Look 2, maybe just cool the fuck down some, bro."

"You two are un-fuckin'-believable," 2 Piece growls. "Especially you." He shoves his finger into my chest harshly, emphasizing his point. "I figured that out of everyone, you'd be the one to have my fuckin' back the most."

"Fuck, man," I shake my head. "Of course I have your back. I also have to think of the club though, not just about you and Avery."

2 Piece flings his arm out. "Is that what this shit is really 'bout? I have her cunt, but you don't?"

Cain looks at me and shakes his head, "Not 'bout to get in the middle of this shit here, bro." He grumbles and walks to the picnic bench. He steps up on the seat to sit on the actual table part. The brothers won't want any part of this fight if they hear what's going on. I can't blame Cain for stepping out of it.

"You know that bullshit isn't true." My eyebrows raise as my temper starts to build. Just because I wear a smile on my face toward him sometimes, don't mean that a fuckin' demon don't still live inside. Trust that shit is still there, just waiting for the wrong motherfucker to piss me off enough to let him come out and play. "This has nothing to do with her ass."

"Oh no? It ain't 'cause I get that pussy every night? Funny 'bro, I see the way you fuckin' look at her."

"For fuck's sake, 2 Piece, I don't know what's gotten into you, but I suggest you clean that shit up real quick. You're not only bein' a fuckin' prick to your brothers, but now you startin' to disrespect a little lady that damn well don't fuckin' deserve to have no one talkin' 'bout her like that."

"You *suggest*, huh? I get it that you're the fuckin' Enforcer and all, but last time I checked, I wear a fuckin' patch too. Doesn't that count for shit anymore 'round here?"

We're interrupted by a throat clearing as Prez walks up behind us. "2 Piece, have you looked at Ares patch lately, brother? You've been in this weird fuckin' funk, you been too busy to notice fuck else. As of the vote this mornin' this here is the new vice president of the Oath Keepers MC, and you are out here talkin' to him out of your fuckin' ass. I don't know what's goin' on with you or if Avery has anything to do with it, but you need to fix your shit brother and congratulate your VP."

"Avery ain't got a motherfuckin' thing to do with this. It's about Twist chasin' after my fuckin' baby sister. I warned every mother-fucker at the table to leave my sister alone."

"I hate to say it, but that's between Twist and Sadie. We don't need no fuckin' drama around here, 2 Piece, and you need to get your shit straight with Ares."

2 Piece clenches his jaw but nods. At least he remembers to show the President some respect. I don't know what's gotten into him. He never acts this way toward me, and I have no idea what the fuck to think of it.

2 Piece turns, still angry, but walks away. As he passes the picnic table he glares at Cain. "The fuck you lookin' at, bitch boy?"

"Bro, I'll fuck you and that little attitude up real fuckin' fast," Cain spits back, and I rush to the table to break up the huge disaster about to happen. Cain will fucking murder 2 Piece with his fists if he gets angry enough.

"Yo, 2! Calm the fuck down!" I glare, standing in front of him with my muscles fully flexed and ready for who the fuck knows at this point.

His eyes flare, and he shoves into my chest angrily.

I can't help myself; I grab him by his throat with one hand, lifting him off the ground. Growling, I storm forward until his back slams into the brick wall of the clubhouse. His blue eyes widen in shock when he makes impact and the air whooshes out of his mouth.

I hold his taut body against the wall, one of my forearms pressed into his chest, the other wrapped tightly around his tattooed neck.

Leaning in close to his ear, I feel his hot breath panting against the side of my face. "Calm. The. Fuck. Down," I hiss. I can't help taking in a deep breath as I'm assaulted with his smell.

For fuck's sake, I'm going to Hell for being so fucking turned on right now. I adjust, moving my legs a little, so no one can see my rock hard dick straining against my jeans. If I had my way right now I'd fuck him so goddamn hard, he wouldn't be able to walk for a week straight, then I'd shove my dick in his mouth to teach him not to talk to me like he's lost his ever loving fucking mind.

After a few minutes, he takes a deep cleansing breath. His body finally relaxes a little, shoulders deflating. His sapphire-colored eyes glance to me, hurt and confusion awash inside his irises. He gazes at me as if *I'm* the one who has betrayed *him*, but all I've done is craved to have him.

"Everything will fucking be okay," I mumble, attempting to show him some compassion, but I suck at that sort of thing. He blinks, the shutters coming up and he nods.

"Yep. My bad. Guess I should say thanks for calming me down and bake you a fuckin' cookie now."

I release him, backing away. I get it. He's pissed, and I probably embarrassed him by manhandling him, but I'm fucking done with his little attitude.

Cain comes to stand beside me, and I silently beg my dick to go down. Cain knows I'm kinky and shit, that I like other things sexually. I'm closest to him, and I don't want him knowing 'bout the shit I really struggle with daily.

2 Piece shakes his head, staring at the ground, then meets Cain's gaze. "Sorry 'bout that, Cain. Didn't mean to get so fuckin' heated. I know this ain't your shit an' all."

"Look, it's cool, bro. I'd probably flip the fuck out if I had a sister I pretty much raised, dating an outlaw biker too." Cain brushes it off and fist bumps 2 Piece. I guess he would be the most understanding, as he goes crazy and fights people quite frequently.

2 Piece nods, clearly still distracted and straightens his clothes out, quickly taking off to go inside the clubhouse.

I take a deep breath, sighing and glancing back at the Prez to find him staring at me curiously. *Shit.* I hope he didn't catch anything more than what Cain did, but I have a feeling he just figured out something. Prez is way too smart and observant, part of the reason why he makes such a good President to a bunch of hard ass bikers.

"What was that all about, Ares?"

"Your guess is as good as mine." I play it off, shrugging. I know what it was, though. He's pissed at Twist and with the crazy tension between 2 Piece, Avery and me since the last time we were together. It's making all three of us a little irritable.

"I thought y'all were close an' all?" Cain peeps up.

"What's that supposed to mean?"

Prez lightly slaps me on the back. "Son, you know what he means. You, Avery, and 2 have a different sort of closeness. I know Cain is your boy and that you're family to me, but they are different for you."

I glance at him, unsure. I've never let anyone in on anything remotely close to this. Why would I? So they can make fun of me and shit like my father used to? I remember the lines he used to taunt me with as he beat me. I'll never forget that surreal day in the cold basement that changed my entire fucking life.

•••

I was hungry that day. I never ate much, being scrawny, malnourished, and abused regularly. Life was awful with my whore of a mother, but at least I usually had some bread to eat.

With my father, however, I stole what little bits of food I could and ate at my one and only friend's house. If it got too bad, I'd occasionally look in a few dumpsters behind the small restaurant near our shack of a house.

Our creepy, old house was covered in wooden shingles, the white wash paint was worn off in many places, and the wood was slowly rotting away. Weeds and trash littered the yard surrounded with a chain link fence. Not that it mattered. Who'd willingly want to go to a place like that? There were three small concrete steps leading to a shoebox-sized, screened-in front porch. The screens, however, had all been broken and stripped out.

My father liked to sit on that porch and wait for me to come in.

Sometimes I could sneak into a back window, but he usually caught me. His scantily-dressed women would come to the front porch, too, and bring him wads of money. I never understood why they would want to come to our house to give money to someone as awful as my father. Wouldn't you rather give money to nice people?

If the women showed up with little or no money, he would beat them. One nasty looking dark girl came; she was as skinny as me at the time, and he caught her poofy hair on fire when she didn't give him what he wanted. Her screams didn't bother me then, though; I was used to all of the screaming, whether it be from me or someone else.

When it was my turn to experience his wrath, I stopped realizing I was even doing the screaming. It's like I went to a completely different world, escaping and making everything bad disappear. Sometimes when I would bleed a lot, I would imagine I was going to pass out and never wake up again. I wouldn't ever have to feel the pain caused by him again.

I tried to hide the bruises and cuts. The first time my friend's dad saw me, he had freaked out. Dom lied and told his dad that he and I had been jumped by some boys at school. I was so scrawny at the time that his dad had believed him.

That was just one of the many times Dom had lied for me. I had been at his house eating dinner right before I came home and *it* all happened.

I always did my best to be silent and invisible. My father had various "tools" in the basement; some he would use to tie people up to, and others he would utilize to hurt people. I hated that room and did whatever I could to stay away from him and it.

I should have known he'd be there waiting for me. I was sneaking in through the back window close to my room, attempting to be as quiet as possible.

I had just put my feet on the nasty matted old carpet when I was slammed into from the side and shoved into the hallway wall. Old bruises caused pain to shatter throughout my body as I collided with the hard surface.

"OOOMPF!" I let loose an aching gasp, my undernourished body trembling, knowing he's within ten feet of me.

"Sneaky, sneaky! You thought I wouldn't smell you, rat?"

He reached out and snatched my midnight black hair. One trait passed down from my mother. He flung my head forward, causing an ache to splinter up my scalp as he threw me to the floor.

Self-preservation kicked in as I began to crawl, screaming at my limbs to move. My fingertips ached as I clawed at the carpet, attempting to move my frail body.

"Get to the basement! It's time I teach you a lesson about sneaking into my house, faggot."

He followed me and shoved me with his foot as I crept toward the basement door. I knew if I didn't go willingly, he would only make it worse on me. I tried to escape the basement trip once before. I'll never do *that* again; it's amazing I even survived.

I crawled as quickly as I could, knowing if I didn't keep going, he'd kick me...hard. The last time I quit crawling, he'd kicked me a couple times, dragged me to the door, and threw me down the wooden stairs.

Once I got to the basement door, I forced myself to get to my feet. When standing, I now came up to his chin. He hated that I was growing; in fact, the bigger I got, the worse the beatings and "lessons" got. He barely paid attention to me when I was small, save the occasional smacks of his belt for allowing myself to be seen.

I feel the cold metal of the door handle twist against my palm. I know I'm just a few steps from agony, and I feel my stomach churn in dread.

The door opens, and I sit on the first step. I slowly scoot down the stairs on my butt like I always have. It's the only way I can go down them without him kicking me first and making me tumble down.

With each zing of pain against my tailbone as it connects with step after step, a new wave of panic sets in.

I can't possibly handle this. My body is too broken to deal with any more; I don't think I can take anything else. I won't live this time. I know he's going to kill me eventually...maybe tonight. Why does he want to hurt me? Why does he hate me so badly? I know it would be easier to just let him kill me than to live day by day in endless pain. I'm young and I shouldn't ache all the time or worry about chipped teeth or my bones not healing right. I hear Dom's mom talking to his dad about these things. I pretend I don't hear her talk, but I do.

I got to go to school while my mom was alive. I didn't have to stop going until he made me, when my mom was murdered by that fat man.

Discomfort climbs up my back as I collide with another step going down. He's killing me this time; I can feel it. His desire to take my blood and my life radiate like a fog around him.

I only have one step left...only one more to go. This is it; this is the last step I will go down.

One...oh, no...just one more. My heart speeds up rapidly as if I may have a heart attack and I start to pant as panic sets in. The basement air is cool, but my forehead is covered in sweat.

My head feels foggy as I scan over every surface in the dim basement. I don't know it until it happens, but somehow I hit my father. I'd made my way to the freezer before he caught up to me.

I remember gripping the hammer and swinging it; each swing colliding with his jaw. He didn't see it coming. It had never crossed his mind that I'd ever fight back or attempt to escape.

Blinking in shock, I swing the hammer as hard as possible again when he stumbles. I can feel the impact of the hammer connect with his skull—both squishy and hard all at once.

My father falls. His dark eyes like mine widen in shock as he sees me charge for him. Once he hits the ground, I climb over his body, straddling him, swinging the hammer again and again. With each strike, his blood splatters all over my fingers, my hands and arms, my face. Each new blow brings a new spray of the thick crimson liquid, and I can't seem to stop myself. Over and over, I slam the strong metal into his broken skull. I can feel the hate climbing down my arms, feeding into the frenzy of finishing him until he's completely gone and can no longer touch me.

I finally stop, my arms feeling beyond heavy and I don't think I could take another swing if I'd wanted to. Dropping the hammer to my side, I hear it make contact with the concrete floor. The air I'd been holding deep inside my lungs finally escapes in a rush. My chest feels tight and achy and the heaviness soon covered my entire body.

Glancing down, I cherish my stained hands and watch the blood droplets running down my forearms. Instead of being frightened, I rub my hands up and down my arms, coating my skin in his blood as if to empower me. The feeling that washes over me is liberating as I wear the blood of my enemy.

My father no longer moves, but I know I will never be free of him. He terrorizes me in my sleep, and I know he will continue to haunt me in the darkness, even after he's no longer here. His face is missing; just a bloody slop in place of his once evil expression. His body remains intact, so I must do something to stop him. He can't ever hurt me again. I have to figure out a way to make it all go away; *he* has to go away completely.

I gaze around the basement, taking in each of his tools and contraptions of horror until my eyes stop on his miter saw. *Perfect.*

His big, muscular body is extremely heavy as I attempt to drag him over to the saw that rests on the bottom shelf of his bench table. My arm muscles weaken and hurt so badly, but I keep on.

I shift and pull his body, shuffling in small steps as I watch his blood smear along the basement floor. Nothing is going to stop this from happening. After countless methods of torture and agony, it's *his* turn, and I don't care if he can feel it or not. This is for *me*, not *him*.

I drop his ankle, scooting the old saw off the dusty shelf and as near to him as the black cord will allow me to. The extension cord gets me barely close enough to reach his knee. That's okay. I just move his large body closer.

That's how it all began...how I became the Butcher.

I started with his ankle, taking one body part at a time. I pushed that saw blade down...the shrill sound...the grinding and smoking as it sliced through his flesh. I can still feel the way the warm blood felt as it sprayed over me.

Dom knows, but not really. He found me that night in the basement. He had never come to my house before, but his father had told him I should stay with them from now. His dad was tired of seeing me hurt, and this was his way of offering me freedom from my father. His father had no idea that I'd created my own stairway to light...to my own escape.

I worked tirelessly cleaning and scrubbing up the gruesome mess I'd left in the basement, just like my father had made me clean up all of the bloody messes before that. As I sprayed disinfectant and dabbed at the last bits of blood, I wiped them away, and I laughed.

I fucking laughed because I had overcome such torture, that I was awash in his own blood this time, and *I* was the one still alive.

I moved in with Dom until I was old enough to find the Oath Keepers MC. We never spoke of that night; in fact, he pretended it never even happened in the first place. I, on the other hand, replayed that shit over in my mind every goddamn day of my life, smiling inside at the fact that fucker was dead and gone.

••••

"Son? You okay, boy?" Prez's gruff voice rouses me.

"I'm not a boy, old man."

"And I ain't no fuckin' old man, so I guess we're even." He chuckles.

Grinning slightly, I nod.

Prez was the first person to really draw me out of my shell. He knew what I needed, being young and confused. He could sense the anger inside, the need for blood occasionally to help keep the beast dormant. He would have me fight sometimes, especially with all of the working out I was doing. I bulked up quickly. I was damn near living in the gym when we first met. The lifting and running helped keep me from wanting to slaughter anyone who made a stupid remark or snide comment in my direction. They had no clue the type of person they were talking about, what I had been through, and what I had to overcome in order to survive.

"I was askin' if you're all right. You seemed far off for a whole minute. I remember what that glazed look means, Ares." He grasps my shoulder in an affectionate squeeze. I tower over the older man, but he doesn't worry. He's shown me nothing but kindness. "Cain and I know 'bout you carin' for Avery and 2 Piece. Maybe you ought to talk to them 'bout it?"

"Nah, I'm good."

"This shit ain't good to hold in, Ares."

"I'm not discussing this with you or with Cain," I declare, my gaze shifting between both of them.

Cain studies me, worriedly. "I'm here, brother."

"Yeah, and it's my own fuckin' shit. If my dick shrinks up, I'll be sure to find you."

"All right, bro, we get it," Cain mumbles and Prez nods.

I can't believe we're even having a conversation about this, for fuck's sake. They should know nothing about this. Prez and Cain don't really have a clue just how much I care for Avery and 2 Piece. At least I hope they don't.

I believe 2 Piece has feelings for me. I could see it in his upset eyes just now. He's confused and I need to talk to him about it, but not yet. He needs to calm down.

Once I speak about it with him, I can finally talk things over with Avery and see where her feelings are. I like to be up front and forward with her. Hell, if I even make it as far as getting to talk to her. I can see 2's emotions bubbling up to the surface, but he's stubborn as fuck and this could turn into something huge if I don't approach him carefully.

Fuck I don't even know the right way to talk about any of this with either of them. I automatically assume they will just accept me into their lives, and I don't even have a clue if they care about me like I care about them.

I think deep inside, I do mean something to Avery. The way she kisses me makes me feel like I'm fucking flying. I get why 2 Piece calls her free bird; she gives you everything you need and yet you still have a serene feeling of freedom, like flying. Not to mention each time I'm inside her, it feels like fucking bliss.

"So are we havin' the BBQ to celebrate still?" Cain inquires while rubbing his muscular stomach. Damn dude is always thinking about food. Surprised he isn't three hundred pounds by now, with all of the muffins and junk he and London are always eating. He can eat more than me, and I'm like five inches taller than the brother.

Prez nods. "Tomorrow we'll all celebrate! You boys deserve it." He grins and walks back inside the clubhouse.

"I still can't believe I got patched Enforcer this morning. To witness you take it off of your cut and then hand it to me was fuckin' awesome. It means more coming from you, knowing you think I'm up for it. Thank you, brother, I know you had a hand in this."

"Cain, it was all you. You earned that patch. In fact, let's take Scratch out. You can break that new patch in and we can scare the shit outta the Prospect."

He laughs and shakes his head. "Can't right now. I called London after church to tell her the news. She told me to get the fuck home to celebrate our own way."

"Ah, sounds fun. Have a good one then. I'm gonna hit up the bar and maybe see if Spin feels like inkin' me since I dipped out last week at the party."

"Bet. I'll see ya tomorrow then."

"Ride safe, brother."

"Yep, be easy."

AVERY

the next day

"**L**ONDON, I STILL CAN'T BELIEVE CAIN LET YOU DRIVE HIS car."

"Did I say he *let* me drive it?" She peers at me curiously.

"No fucking way! You took his car? Are you nuts?"

She shrugs, wearing a shit-eating grin and turns to walk into the grocery store. She's lost her freaking mind. Cain is going to redden her ass like no tomorrow, and I bet she's anticipating just that.

"This right here is why we're such good friends. You know that, right?" I chortle loudly, walking quickly to catch up with her long legs.

"Because we both like to steal cars?" Her icy blue irises sparkle and I giggle.

"No, but this is pretty epic. I wonder if he's figured it out yet."

"Oh my phone will be blowing up like crazy when he does. Don't worry, we'll know."

"You don't think he would come here on his bike, do you? He still keeps his old bike at the club, right?"

"Fuck my life. If you see him, hide. I need to have a cake or something in my hands when he sees me. I know I can distract him if I promise he can lick something off of me."

"And I thought *I* was the kinky one."

"Please, bitch. You are *so* the kinky one! Speaking of, how is the deal working out with having Ares too?" She glances at me as she gets a shopping cart and starts walking toward the produce section in the grocery store.

"I don't have Ares too." I gaze at her a little confused.

I've shared some small details about what 2 Piece and I have worked out with Ares, but she doesn't know the extent of it. No one, and I mean absolutely no one, can know just how much I really enjoy it. I don't want anything to jeopardize what I have with 2 Piece. I've never been so happy in my entire life as I am here with him.

"You know what I mean. You do have Ares, by the way. You have both of them. It's not just me Avery, everyone can see it."

"Whatever. I have 2 Piece and I'm very happy with that." I roll my eyes, throwing random shit in the cart to make a giant pasta salad for the BBQ the club is putting on this evening.

"Come on, Avery, tell me what it's like to be with the freaking Butcher, of all people!"."

"Shh, don't call him that!"

"Why not? That's what everyone calls him."

"No, London. That's what all the brothers who gossip call him. He's not *a butcher*. He's kind and gentle."

"Ares? Is kind and gentle? He's Mr. Control Freak who looks like this massive pissed off Savage all of the time, and you're telling me he's gentle. Don't get me wrong, Avery, I like Ares a lot. He and Cain are really cool. Cain thinks of him as his closest brother, but it's hard to think of him as anything but some of the horror stories I've heard whispered through the clubhouse."

"Since when are you one to gossip? Usually you're the one getting onto me about minding my own business."

"I know, and I'm sorry about that. I guess no one really knows much about Ares besides the Prez. Ares is quiet and grouchy most of the time. I'm just really curious about him. I'm close to most of the brothers, but he keeps his distance."

Huffing, I nod. "I know. I'm sorry for jumping down your throat. I just feel protective of him for some reason. He's my friend, and I care about him."

"You feel protective over the club's badass Enforcer turned VP? You *do* know he got the nickname 'The Butcher' for a reason, right? Just please be careful with him, okay?"

"I will. I mean it, he's sweet to me."

"Good, I'm glad to hear he's good to you. How's 2 Piece deal with it all anyhow? I get that he used to be a playboy and all, but I would think he would be a little territorial over the one who finally anchored him. Cain said he's been kind of weird, like distant and moody lately."

I load up on some different bags of chips and dip as London strolls through the aisle, pushing the cart beside me.

"Honestly, he *has* been kind of weird and quiet this week. Even with Ares and normally he just jokes around with him. We had this great time together last week and ever since, he's just been kind of lost."

I leave out the part that every time they've been in the same room, I catch 2 Piece staring at Ares like he wants to rip his clothes off and fuck him silly. I'm lost with this and have no clue whatsoever on what to say to either of them. I think Ares is clueless about it all. I only know what that look means because usually I'm the only one 2 Piece ever directs it toward.

I follow London to the check-out line. Prez gave us a wad of money to 'get some BBQ shit together' and hopefully we got everything he wanted. We pretty much picked up everything besides the kitchen sink.

I busy myself helping unload the cart. Pickles go on the conveyor belt, ketchup—Ares licking up my spine. I blink and set the mayo down next, hamburger buns—Ares tying my ripped shirt over my eyes. I breathe in deeply and huff as I drop a bag of chips remembering what it felt like to have them both in me at the same time. I always feel

50

the most complete inside when I have them both like that. I know it's wrong. I love 2 Piece so much. I would die for him if I ever needed to.

I've been screwed from the very start but just hadn't realized it until we all became intimate together. I can deny it all I want, but it does no good. That first night he caught me in the hallway, I remember thinking he was going to kill me and then he put his fingers inside of me. My world tilted, and I've quietly watched him ever since.

Ares and I became friends and I had a little bit of a crush on him, I think. Sort of like the Beast from that Disney movie. The closer to him you get, the kinder he becomes. I think his idea of giving a woman a library is tying her up with belts and making her happy in a whole other way.

Now I'm stuck. I know I should stop asking 2 Piece to invite Ares into the bedroom with us, but I can't seem to stop. Imagine you getting your first refreshing drink of spring water and then attempting to never drink it again. *Fuck.* I surely can't feel that strongly about him. It's not right. You don't fall for two men, and you can't have two men, at least not to keep.

I shake my head, loading the full white plastic bags into the cart. I have to stop this nonsense. I won't cause problems with 2 and his brothers or in my relationship. 2 Piece has been more than enough for me to handle. Surely I can get back there with a little time away from Ares.

London and I head to Cain's black Challenger. She pushes the cart and uses the little plastic clicker to open the trunk.

"Look, Avery, I'm sorry for crossing the line earlier. Are you okay? You've been really quiet, and silence isn't normally your strongest feature."

I burst out laughing. Looking at her, I can't help it. She's completely right. I'm normally a pretty big chatterbox. "I'm okay. Just thinking over some stuff. I'll be fine, especially tonight. We have a party to plan!"

"Yes ma'am, it's gonna be so much fun! I love having the brothers together and making good food. I hope to God Smile's decided to smoke a brisket. I wish my brother would come around and get to know the club too, but he's stubborn." She's told me about him before, I guess some chick pulled a doosie on him not to long ago and he's been pretty depressed. I hate that she worries about him.

"Oh my God, that brisket is fucking amazing!"

"Hell yeah!" She smiles widely. "I'm going to go put the cart up."

"Okay, lady." I nod, shifting the groceries around the large trunk space so I can close the trunk properly. That's how you know we bought a lot of food; Cain's trunk is so big, he could probably fit a few bodies back here if he needed. Ugh, I don't want to even imagine that one. Once I shut the lid, I glance up and jump, startled.

I bring my hand to my chest, my breath accelerating when I see the man waiting for me silently a few feet away. He has short black hair and bright green eyes, his face marred with a scar. It looks like someone stuck a knife in his mouth and sliced his cheek so he has a half permanent smile scar. It's totally freaky.

"Umm, can I help you?" I ask and make my way around the car, placing the vehicle between us and not taking my eyes off of him. I remember the last time I ran into a Twisted Snake MC member not too long ago and got shot in my leg because of it. I want some sort of protection between him and me.

He grins, following me on his side of the vehicle toward the front where I'm now positioned.

"Yes'em, you can help all right." The way he says it, brings chills to my skin and I swallow nervously.

There's nothing really between us anymore, we're face-to-face in front of the hood of the car.

"What do you want?" I suck up my nerves and question—bravely or otherwise—drawing on any bit of courage I have inside.

"You tell that rotten fuckin' President of yours that we heard he has a new VP. Tell him we fuckin' remember what happened to the real VP and he better get ahold of us."

"You leave the VP alone." I prop my hand on my hip, cocking it out a little and glaring spitefully. "I don't know who the hell you think you are or where you get the balls to threaten my club and vice president, but you seriously need to back off."

His eyebrow lifts and he grins an evil smirk, "That right? *Your* club? Huh. You close to this new VP?"

He steps closer to me and my eyes widen in panic. He's way bigger than me. He could probably squash me with his boot and yet my dumb ass can't keep my mouth shut for shit. I didn't seem to have any problem being quiet for once in the store, now I'm a goddamn chatter box when it comes to defending Ares.

Luckily, I catch a glimpse of London sneaking up behind him. He lifts his plain heather gray T-shirt up, revealing a blade hidden underneath, leather holster tucked into his pants.

"Look, I'm not telling you anything about anyone. You should just leave before you piss off the club."

Chuckling, he unsnaps his blade and I squeak. London counts with her fingers behind him and when she gets to her third finger she raises her leg up, kicking the shit out of the back of his knee.

He yelps, flinging forward and the only thing I can think to do is grab his head, slamming it into the hood of Cain's car as London continues to kick him anywhere she possibly can.

She kicks him really hard in the kidneys as I'm struggling to hold his head down against the front end. "Fucking run, bitch! Get in the damn car!" She screams, eyes crazy and hair flailing around her like some nutty chick that's ready to commit murder.

I release his sweaty head as he briefly drops to the ground, and then he starts to stand, his stance shaky. I feel my flip flops skid out from underneath me against the asphalt parking lot as I take off, but fuck if I let it slow me down.

I practically leap to the car door, ripping it open at the same time as London. We slam the doors shut and she cranks the loud engine over, the Challenger letting out a mean, nasty growl as it comes to life.

My door suddenly gets pulled open by the crazy man and London floors it as I scream. The tires spin and smoke. I swear we must have come off of the pavement with how hard she slammed down on that gas pedal. The backside of the car whips to the side, digging for traction, and my door swings for a second before it crashes closed as I'm thrown back into my seat.

I'm panting so heavily I may fucking hyperventilate. After a moment my body propels forward, flying toward the dashboard as London slams on the brakes.

"I don't think so, motherfucker!" she hisses, turning the car in a one eighty and speeding back through the grocery store parking lot toward the scary looking man.

She clips him with the right front fender, his body making an audible thump as if we just ran over a large rabbit in the road.

"Holy shit, London! What the fuck are you doing? You can't run him over. You will go to fucking jail, dude!"

"The hell I will. Cain won't let that fucker talk!" she declares, flooring it again, this time toward the clubhouse.

London turns the stereo up. It blares "Lydia" by Highly Suspect so loudly, my nose hairs vibrate each time the bass resonates.

I can see her arms visibly shaking as she clutches the steering wheel with both hands. She looks like she's holding on for dear life, and I have a feeling if she were to let go of it, she would probably lose control and wreck the damn car.

We fly over the little hills on the old highway, and my nerves are dangling by a thread as I grip the oh shit handle tightly. Fuck, I could use some type of drug right now, and I don't do drugs! I didn't even do wild shit like this when I partied in college. *I can't believe she just hit someone with the fucking car!*

London takes the turn to the clubhouse and the tires spin out as they meet the small gravel road leading to the compound entrance. She lays on the horn, blaring it when the gate comes into sight, and I lean forward bracing myself by holding onto the dash. It looks like this bitch is about to fly through the fucking gate if it isn't opened. For the love of all things holy, Prez is going to kick our asses, I swear.

"London!" I call out, closing my eyes tightly, waiting for the impact to happen.

The car turns sharply and the tires screech as London slams on the brakes and I'm suddenly thrown into my door like I'm on one fucked up roller coaster ride.

London flings the car shifter into park as tears start to stream down her face. "I'll be damned if some fuckhead thinks he'll take me away from my baby. I'm pregnant and fuck if I don't get to make it here to tell Cain before some douche canoe thinks he can come along and screw up my life!"

My stomach lurches as I hear her confession on why she went looney in the grocery store parking lot, running the guy over. I swallow and nod, then wrench my door open. I turn to stand, but my shaky legs fail me and I drop to the ground, puking all over the floor in front of me.

I just wanted some fucking BBQ today.

ARES

SCRATCH STARTS BLOWING UP MY PHONE ABOUT CAIN TEAR-ing down the drive and damn near taking out the gate. I don't know what the fuck he's talkin' about since Cain is sitting right next to me, sippin' his whiskey and lemon, preaching to me about some kind of fuckin' vitamin I should take. I hang up on Scratch and gesture for Cain to follow me. I don't know what the fuck is going on, so I take out my Glock just in case.

"Yo, Cain, Scratch is fucking trippin', said you just blew through the fuckin' gate."

"What the fuck, bro? Has he gone off his rocker?" Cain glances at me confused. "I haven't left. I spoke to the dude on my way through the gate earlier."

Shrugging, I nod to the door. "I don't know, brother, but be ready, 'cause we gotta go check this shit out."

"Ares, you're VP now. You stay, and I'll take 2 Piece or another member with me."

"I don't give fuck 'bout that. I'm going. It's what I do. You go and grow a vagina on me?" I'm always giving Cain shit about really being a female since he's all health conscious, bitching at us to 'make better choices' and shit when we eat.

"Fuck off. You know my dick's bigger." Cain smirks and follows me.

2 Piece jumps up when he sees us rushing toward the door. "Sup?"

"Scratch gibbering on about fuck knows." I shrug, replying gruffly and keep walking to the door.

2 unclips his pieces from their holsters and follows us quickly. One thing I admire about him is that he's always ready to back us up, even if it's the last thing he wants to do.

I crash through the club door momentarily blitzed by the bright sun light, blinking quickly to get my focus. Cain and 2 Piece come charging through behind me.

Sure as fuck, Cain's beauty, Loretta, is parked vertically in front of the club entrance with one hell of a skid mark trailing.

Avery's hanging out of the passenger side, puking her guts up, and a sobbing London climbs out of the driver side.

"The fuck is going on?" I bellow, trying to appear calm. Inside I'm freaking the fuck out, clearly seeing the girls are so upset.

Cain and 2 Piece each rush to London and Avery, trying to calm their Ol' ladies down. I badly want to follow 2 Piece, to comfort Avery but make myself stay rooted to my spot.

Cain grasps London, pulls her to him, and wraps his arms around her as he rocks back and forth, "Shhh baby...shhh... tell me what's wrong, and I'll fuck 'em up. Talk to me, London, come on baby."

She winds her hands in Cain's shirt, burying her face in his neck trying to get her emotions under control. Cain looks so pissed like the brothers' head may pop the fuck off.

I make my way around the car to the opposite side to check if Avery can fill me in. 2 Piece leans over her into the car to grab her drink so she can rinse her mouth out. After she's finished drinking, he helps her stand on her shaky legs.

"Angel, wanna fill me in?" Grumbling, I scan her from head to toe to make sure there's not a scratch on her. I would fucking skin someone alive for touching a hair on her body.

She takes a deep breath and closes her eyes. Staying silent, she makes my heart rate speed up even faster.

"You girls gotta give us something; we need to know what to do." I'm almost ready to beg; I just want to keep her and my club safe by any means necessary.

"Bunch of damn alphas—the lot of you," Sadie pipes up, full of sass. We all turn, noticing her for the first time.

2 Piece's eyes get wide, and he growls, "Were you with them, Sades?"

"Nope, I was out back setting up the BBQ when I heard someone tearing through the drive; I thought I would come make sure everyone was okay."

2 Piece huffs, about to flip his shit, so I step in, "Look little momma, you need to stay out in the back of the club if shit's goin' down; we want you safe. Now, do you know what happened?"

"No. Like I said, I just came and saw them like that," she nods toward London and Avery.

"Thanks, momma. How 'bout you go relax and take care of that babe, yeah?"

She raised her eyebrow at all of us, nodded, and then headed to the back yard.

"I had that," 2 Piece huffs, irritated.

"I know man, but it's different if I suggest it, versus her feelin' like you're ordering her around."

"Yeah, good point."

"Avery, talk to me." I murmur, softer.

"Well," she breaths deeply, "we had an issue at the grocery store."

Cain growls, "What kind of fuckin' issue?"

2 Piece throws his hands up. "That's it, you're not going to that fucking grocery store again! I'm done! Have one of the other bitches go, but you've had nothin' but bullshit at that fuckin' place."

Cain nods, "Yep, you too, baby, no more fuckin' shopping."

"I'm pregnant." London responds bluntly, wiping her cheeks from

58

the leftover tears. We all hold our breath watching the couple.

Cain drops to his knees in the middle of the parking lot, rains kisses all over her shirt-covered stomach and rubs up her thighs as she runs her hands through his dark faux hawk.

2 Piece shakes his head, mumbling, "Christ, Cain's on his way to a damn car load."

We all chuckle, slightly lightening the seriousness of what's going on.

"All right girls, 'nough fucking around, tell me what's going on."

Cain climbs to his feet, holding London from behind so he can rest his hands on her stomach, while he peppers kisses on her neck. 2 Piece takes a step away from Avery, keeping their connection by holding her hand. The women look at me while the men send worried glances their way.

"We were confronted by a guy about the club and were lucky enough to get away. I made sure he couldn't follow us," London mumbled out, attempting to be as monotone as possible, giving me the information that I need to know immediately.

"So, no lockdown right this minute?"

"Close the gate just to make sure." London glances towards the entrance worriedly.

"You got it." I nod, pulling my phone out to text Scratch to secure the gate to the compound.

Cain pulls away, grabbing London's hand and tugging her toward the club. "Come on, sugar tits, tell us all 'bout it inside." She relents, and follows him inside.

I pop open the trunk for the groceries and close the two car doors as Avery and 2 Piece head into the club. I grab the groceries from the trunk and follow them inside.

Once I get inside I send a text to Smiles, telling him to get the club girls to unload the groceries and head straight to the Prez's office. I need to update him on this shit ASAP.

Knocking on the door frame, I pop my head in the open doorway,

"Prez?"

"Yeah son, come on in."

"We need church ASAP, with Avery and London attending."

"Ol' Ladies don't come to church, you know this."

"They were just confronted at the grocery store, and we all need to hear what went down."

"Gotcha, I'll text the boys; be ready in ten."

I nod, leaving the room. I wonder what kind of shit storm this is gonna be.

Cain and London are quietly arguing when I get back to the bar, but I can still make out what they're saying.

"You took Loretta, London? Why didn't you tell me?"

"Cain, Loretta is just a damn car, and thankfully, I was driving her and not my piece of shit Civic. If that guy would have followed me, I never would have outrun him if I wasn't in your car!"

"I get it; I wish you would have said something about it though."

"Why, so you could argue with me about driving it?"

"No baby, so I could get you a new car. Now you're pregnant again, and it gives me an excuse to get you an SUV or something."

"I don't need a new car," she says stubbornly and Cain huffs.

"Woman! Are you trying to drive me crazy on purpose?"

"And what if I am?"

He grabs her quickly, taking her mouth and expressing all of his frustration in an erotic as fuck kiss. God, I wish I could walk up to Avery and kiss her like that when I got irritated 'bout something. Shaking my head, I scan the room for Avery and 2 Piece.

Heading over to my usual booth, they appear to be in their own heated discussion; I'm assuming about her not calling him right away.

"I'm fine Silas, I told you."

"I just can't ever keep you fuckin' safe, Avery. It's fucked up."

I clear my throat, effectively interrupting them. "2 Piece, brother, this shit isn't your fault." I swallow, glancing at Avery. "All that matters is that the girls made it back and unharmed. Prez is gonna call church in a few."

"You're the fucking VP now, Ares, do something about these fucks."

"Calm down, we have to find out everything we can before just jumping all over shit. I know Cain is gonna be foaming at the mouth for this fuck, and I want to find him, too. I'll figure out something, just try an' be patient."

Avery takes a deep breath, following it with a big drink of water. "Well, I guess I should start on making the pasta salad."

2 Piece looks at her incredulously. "The fuck Shorty? Why do you have to brush shit off as if it didn't happen. You're not gonna make no fuckin' salad, you're comin' to church."

"Since when are women allowed in church, 2 Piece? I'm making that damn salad because I just picked out all of the shit for it!"

"Stubborn, I fuckin' swear, Avery."

She glares at him and then turns to me frustrated, seeking help.

"Fighting won't do either of you any good. Shit just went down, so you're coming to tell us all about it, Avery." I glance back to him. "2 Piece, fucking just be grateful she's breathing and not fucking hurt this time," grumble and they both get quiet. I guess the little reminder of her getting shot on the back of his bike awhile back, made them remember shit could always be worse.

The brothers start chuckling and cat calling. Strange since they were nervous about getting to church to hear about what just went down.

"Crazy bitch!" Avery smiles, shaking her head and points behind me.

Turning I'm met with London laying on the bar top, stretched out just like the first time she came to the club house, as Cain pours tequila in her belly button and sprinkles salt on her cleavage. Brently is behind the bar with shot glasses lined up to fill them all with tequila.

After Cain is done getting her ready, he turns to the club, "Brothers! Grab a shot and celebrate the best news all day. My baby is knocked up!" He finishes by sucking the tequila from her belly button, causing

61

London to grin a Cheshire smile. The brothers send out a room full of congratulations and excited whistles as they pass around the shots.

Once we get ours, we each tap glasses and swallow down the strong gold liquor. At least he picked something with a little kick; today in church, I think we're damn sure going to need it.

Prez strolls in moments later, congratulating London and Cain, and then gets straight into business, calling church.

We all file in to the chapel and take our respective seats. This is the first time I'm sitting right next to the Prez, as the official Vice President of my club. I thought I would be nervous, but surprisingly, I feel confident. I've helped the club as the Enforcer for years, and I know I will be able to help them as VP as well.

Cain sits directly next to me now, in my old seat. It's a little surreal, but I'm glad it's his body filling that chair. 2 Piece moves up to sit in Cain's old spot, across the table next to Smiles, our Road Captain. 2 Piece isn't the club Brawler like Cain used to be, that's not why he filled that seat. He moved spots because it's all about the pecking order. The closer you are to the Prez's spot, the higher the patch you wear. 2 Piece now handles all of the weapons aspects for the club's personal and business uses.

I have to say, it's refreshing to see the people I'm closest to move up in ranks with me. It will make my job easier in the long run. Fuck knows we don't want to have to worry about another traitor at the table, like the old brother, Capone.

"Brothers, one thing that needs to be announced is that we had previously voted on 2 Piece getting patched as the club's new Sergeant at Arms. Well, he agreed to it, and it's now official." The room explodes in cheers, ribbing, and congratulating 2 Piece on the new spot he holds.

Once all the commotion dies down, Prez moves on to what happen-ed at the store. It's not less important than the patch announcement, it was just older business, and Prez always attempts to handle club shit in the order it happens.

The girls sit against the wall in the extra folding chairs and when we're ready for them, they recite the events from the grocery store so all the brothers can hear what happened. I notice Twist getting a little crazy eyed when he hears the girls talking about the guy showing them his knife and how they defended themselves in order to get away.

We're all very lucky the bastard didn't have time to get his knife out and really hurt the girls. Nonetheless, they're shaken up, and I know it's eating all of the brothers up inside to not have this piece of filth here to torture.

The Prez takes a large drink of water, looking peeved, his wrinkles more pronounced with stress. "Do you have any idea on who the fuck it could be? Did they have any patches on that look like the Twisted Snakes? Or any patches at all that could help us?"

Avery shakes her head, still a little pale from being sick and then having to rehash it all. "No, Prez. I'm sorry, I didn't even think about that. I was just so scared when he started talking about the new VP. I just couldn't help but tell him to leave the VP and the club alone. I know I shouldn't have said anything at all."

"Aww shug', ain't nothin' to be sorry for. You girls did the right thing and I know it's not only me who's proud, but all the brothers here are proud of how you two handled the situation." He nods, pointing at Avery and London. "Our main concern is keepin' y'all safe and getting you out of that situation. Y'all showed us that if needed, you can work together and really fuck someone up. Not only did you do it to protect yourselves, but you did it to stand up for this club."

The brothers all nod pleased, looking at London and Avery with a higher level of respect. I swear my chest swells with pride when I hear how she stood up for me and how they took care of the ass face who was bothering them. Not only are our brothers not to be fucked with, but obviously our women are baddasses, too.

2 Piece leans forward, anger simmering in his blue gaze, "'Bout that...the fuck we doin' to catch this sicko?" he hisses, ready to get his

revenge.

Twist grins wickedly, "I'll ride through town."

Twist is so fucked up, I know he has to be jonesin' for some blood by now; it's been a while since he's gotten to play with anyone. I think having 2 Pieces sister, Sadie, around here is good for him. She's kept Twist occupied. He acts like an old lady fretting over her pregnant self and shit. I still don't know what happened with her or why she came to the club. 2 Piece and Twist went to Cali to find her baby daddy and didn't come back with shit.

Prez shakes his head, "Naw Twist, you sit tight, brother. We need to figure out who this is before we pop off hurtin' random people."

2 Piece demands, glaring, "This is fuckin' bullshit. We should be out lookin' for this scum!"

Prez glances at me, irritated with 2 Piece's outburst. Taking a deep breath, I peer over at 2, "Brother, we'll figure this shit out and find him, I promise."

2 Piece rolls his eyes at me, huffing in disbelief. In that moment all I can think about is slamming him against a wall, face first and taking him hard. I'd wipe that little look off his face and make him give into me; make him believe every word I say. He'd listen once he figured out who was really in control.

I understand he's pissed, but we have to be smart about this shit. We don't need any cops or feds breathing down our fuckin' throats if we start getting sloppy. If that happens, we'll get nowhere in finding this person.

Prez stretches, rubbing the back of his neck as he thinks up a plan. "I understand everyone's fuckin' pissed. Smiles, hit up the other Captains around; see if anyone's tryin' to move in." He looks down to the end of the table at the NOMADS, "Nightmare, Exterminator, since you boys are still here, keep your ears open in those little bars y'all like to chill at." They both chin lift, and Exterminator grunts.

Prez nods, "Cain, you and Twist go to the grocery store the girls were at. See if anyone's hangin' around, and see if you can get some surveillance tapes."

"On it." Cain answers immediately, excited to be one step closer to getting London's tormentor.

"What about me and 2 Piece?"

"Ares, they seem real keen on our fuckin' VP." Prez looks a little shaken up about the whole VP thing and I have no idea why. You'd think he'd be more upset about the girls being confronted on club shit. "I want you to stay close," he mutters.

Prez turns to 2 Piece, "You're gonna get in touch with our weapons contacts. I want you to make sure our orders are full and we're in good standing with them all. I don't give a fuck if you have to ride out to visit them all, just get it done."

2 Piece nods, quietly fuming inside. I'm sure he's pissed he's not tasked with riding street by street looking for someone to hurt. I wish he wasn't dealing with this so he could appreciate getting a spot at the table with a title. This should be a time of celebrating; who knows if he even really wants it. You'd think with Avery causing him to settle down some, he'd want to move up in the ranks. Instead, we're faced with more fucking club drama.

Twist is now in the next spot to move up and fuck knows if he could deal with it. I'm surprised he's still alive with all the risks he likes to take. Motherfucker is pretty *twisted* up inside.

"Umm, excuse me," Avery interrupts politely, and we all quiet, turning to her, surprised, "So are we still having the BBQ today?"

"Well shug', do you feel up to it?"

"Yes, we got a ton of food, and I'd like to cook it. Ares, Cain, and 2 Piece deserve to celebrate their new patches, don't y'all agree?"

Prez nods, a little taken back at her speaking up for the brothers getting patches. She just keeps fitting more and more into the club. Maybe it's good she's around London a lot. She'll teach Avery what all is expected and she'll fit perfectly amongst us. "Yep, they sure the fuck do, sugar. You got it; we can party tonight after everyone gets their shit straight."

She smiles brightly, her face gaining some color back, and you'd never guess her life was practically threatened earlier. Avery is quickly evolving into a ride-or-die chick, and that shit makes me want her even more. God, she's fucking beautiful. I wish I could have her; hell, I wish I could have her and 2 Piece both.

Church gets dismissed shortly after and I'm left questioning more than before. Why the fuck did Prez get antsy about hearing that the guy was talking about our club's new VP? I know we're close, but normally he would just roll with it; instead, he wants me to stay cooped up at the club? Something just doesn't feel right, and I'm going to have to dig a little deeper.

Pretty much everyone is on their phones when we hit the bar. 2 Piece storms off toward his room, and both girls head to the kitchen. I'm guessing they plan to start prepping the food for tonight. I really don't know what the fuck to do. This is a first. I'm usually busy taking care of something and making sure the guys are all checking in.

I feel virtually useless without having any tasks to complete or leading a search, and it angers me. My blood starts to boil, thinking about that asshat who threatened Avery and then threatened the club. I want to hurt anyone who dares to try any of it. Those thoughts soon evolve over to 2 Piece and him rolling his fucking eyes at me. And in the middle of fucking church of all places. It keeps replaying in my mind like a song I can't shake, feeding into my craving to teach him a lesson.

I crack my knuckles and then my neck; I've had enough of his fucking attitude lately. Heading down the hallway towards his and Avery's room, I open the door straight away, 'cause fuck knocking at this point; I have shit to say, and he's gonna listen.

We've been in this fucked up type of relationship or whatever you want to call it since last month. I've wanted them both from the very start, and it's been a fuckin' year since Avery started popping in for visits with 2 Piece.

Lily's ears perk up when she sees me enter; she jumps up off her fluffy, tan dog bed to great me with puppy kisses. "Easy girl," I mumble. I scratch her soft belly for a few moments as she rolls on her back on the carpet.

I hear the shower going, so I know he must be in there. His clothes are scattered everywhere, even though the rest of his room is immaculate. 2 Piece is a huge neat freak, almost to the point of OCD with some shit.

My stomach twirls inside, picturing him in the shower, completely naked. I'm fucking sick and tired of not having him. It's time I show him I run this fuckin' show. Peeling my clothes off and throwing them in the chair, I vibrate with need, excited to see his sexy tattooed body again.

Once I'm ready, I take a deep breath and make my way to the small bathroom. Opening the cheap contractor grade door, a burst of steam escapes around me, instantly warming my flesh. I can make out his muscular outline through the foggy shower enclosure.

After a moment, his body stiffens, probably noticing the rush of cool air. I take the first step, waiting for him to say something. When he remains silent, I move a few more steps, opening the shower door. It creaks loudly and he turns, facing me, eyes widening in alarm. His body is soapy, covered in white suds from the plain bar he holds in one of his hands. The clean smell surrounds me, and I can't help but to get even further turned on.

"Ares? 'Sup, brother?"

I witness his sapphire eyes scan over my naked flesh from head to toe, finally meeting my dark gaze, his expression brimming with many questions.

Good, I'm glad I caught him off guard. "I can't control it any longer." Licking my lips, I clench my hands into fists. "I've tried to stomp it down, I've attempted to put it off. No more. You're fuckin' mine 2 and I'm all outta' waitin' for your ass." Gritting sternly, I step into the shower stall with him.

He shifts over a step, as my large body eats up most of the room.

"What are you doing?" Mumbling, he rubs his hand over the muscles on his stomach, drawing attention to his semi-hard cock.

"You know what I'm doing," I retort softly. "You know inside what it is that I want. You crave it, too. I can see it written all over your face each time I'm around you." I graze his scruffy jaw, and he turns away from my touch.

"No, Ares, its fuckin' wrong." Shaking his head, he attempts to make excuses. "I don't know what it is I want when we're around each other; my thoughts are scattered. I either feel like I hate you or I want you or it just confuses the fuck outta me." Glancing at me, he skirts over my body again, and then turns to stare out of the shower glass. "I can't even believe you're in here. What if Avery comes in here? Then what?"

"Don't worry about Avery; I'll take care of it."

"No, I'm not fucking up the one good thing in my life."

"2?"

"Huh?" He turns back to me, meeting my gaze.

"I ain't fuckin' askin' you shit."

He huffs and I do exactly what I came here to do. I take control. I bear it all on me, because he needs to be able to let go and blame his feelings and actions on me. I tower over him, taking notice of his stiff cock. He wants me just as fuckin' much as I want him.

Quickly, I twist him so his back is facing me. I brace my arm across his chest like a clamp, making him unable to move his arms. If he really wanted out he could kick me or flail, but he just jerks a few times until I take his dick in my other hand. Pumping it from tip to base a few times, he stiffens up.

"What?" He stutters out surprised. "No Ares, we can't do this."

I keep going, driving on and after a moment his shoulders drop and his head falls forward, taking in the pleasure. He can try to fight it, but his body screams that he wants it. He just needs a little push; he needs to realize it does feel as good as he imagines it would.

Murmuring against his neck, I coax it out of him, "You want this. I know, because I want it. God, I want it so bad, 2 Piece."

"I can't want it," he gasps, as I continue to stroke him.

"I'm not giving you any choice this time; I want you too badly. You can try and fight it, but your body doesn't lie."

"My body doesn't know what it wants."

Releasing his cock, I use the pump bottle beside me, filling my hand with Avery's conditioner. Once I have enough, I reach below, using it as lubrication for his tight entrance.

I work a few fingers into him, pumping, as his chest rises and falls quickly.

"The fuck it doesn't. You push your ass into my hand because you want me to take it. You can fight it, but like it or not, you're already mine."

"Fuck, why does it have to feel so good?" he croons out on a small moan.

"Because it's with me."

Removing my fingers, I line the head of my cock to his entrance. Slowly, I work the tip of myself into him, but have to pull out due to the resistance. I absolutely love the fact that he's all mine this way. Using a little more conditioner, I push myself into him enough so I can thrust my dick in deeply. He groans low, trying to quiet himself through the pain.

"This is going to hurt you more than it does me right now. I'm going to fuck you like I've wanted to. Later it will get easier. Through the pain you will find pleasure, and I'll make sure you cum."

I push into him fully again and he gasps, fists clenching in pain. He groans, and I plunge my way into him for a fourth time, finally releasing his arms after a moment.

"Lean forward and brace yourself against the wall."

"This is wrong," he weakly croaks as I grip his hips. He's opened up enough now that I can powerfully drive into him.

"Ah, fuck!" he lets out loudly, and I reach around and grab his cock again.

With each strong, amazing drive into his tightness, I pump his stiff cock at the same time.

"I told you 2 Piece, I'm fuckin' done. No more pussy footin' around. I want you both; you and Avery, even more so than what we've been doin'."

He grunts, moaning through my deep drive into him, and then gasps, "Fuck! God that hurts so bad, but feels so fuckin' good." Reaching down, he wraps his hand over mine, holding it as I stroke him. "What will Avery think if she sees us like this?" he asks brokenly.

"She'll love it," I whisper against the shell of his ear. "She wants it just as badly as we do; she fuckin' has too, because I can't not be able to have you." I lean over him, thrusting in and kiss up his back. His dick starts to throb in my hand, and it pushes me on toward the brink.

"Oh you like that, huh? You like my tongue on you? I can't wait to have it all over this fucking body," I mutter.

He raises from his bent over stance, standing up, his back snuggly against my chest, as I tenderly kiss and suck on his neck as I continue pumping into him. 2 Piece reaches back, gripping tightly onto one of my thick thighs. To feel his large, strong grip on my skin makes me erupt like a goddamn geyser.

"Fuuuuck," I call in a deep, low moan against his neck as I clamp my eyes shut. "I'm coming. You feel so fucking tight, so fucking hot."

As my words spill out in ecstasy, 2 Piece follows, spurting his warm, thick cum all over my hand and groaning. I finish with my release, lightly kissing his shoulder and take a step back.

He turns finally and faces me with a look of guilt on his face.

"Stop it, don't fuckin' ruin perfection," I grumble. I take his cheek in my large palm, and I do what I've been aching to do each time I catch him close to me.

I lean in and take his lips, thrusting my tongue into his mouth. I kiss him thoroughly, and he doesn't fight me for control. Instead, he gives in and takes everything I give him. Besides Avery, it's the best fucking kiss I've ever had in my life. I could probably come just from kissing him long enough.

I finally pull away, and he gazes at me almost in awe. I know he had to feel how perfect that was. I bend toward him again and kiss him chastely before I step out of the shower, leaving him speechless. That couldn't have been any more perfect for me; he felt like pure bliss. I'm pretty sure he's convinced that it's not just a thing anymore, that he's meant to be with not only Avery, but with me, too.

Drying off with the small, light blue towel, my body's thoroughly satisfied for the moment. I'm about to leave the bathroom when he finally speaks up, breaking the silence.

"We have to talk about this. I won't keep this from her," he grumbles, his arms braced against the glass door as he peers through it at me.

"Good, I would never expect you to. Oh and, 2 Piece? You let her know I'm coming for her next."

2 PIECE

one week later

WELL WE STILL HAVEN'T FOUND THAT FUCK HEAD THAT upset the girls at the grocery store, but the club got its first note dropped off in the middle of the night. Scratch found it tied to the gate this morning when he went out to sit in his little post. We always have someone monitoring the gate and who comes and goes into the compound. You never know when you may piss off the wrong person or when the cops might decide to pay us a little visit.

Ares stares at the note again, looking at it like it's written in fucking Chinese or some shit. "So what the fuck are we doin'?" I question, ready to demand a plan of action. He always takes his time with shit, being the smart one about these kinds of things, but I want it squashed now, before it gets even more serious.

The Prez has been gone a lot this week for fuck knows why, so the burden of it all has fallen to Ares' shoulders. I bet he's pretty stressed the fuck out, having all these new responsibilities thrown on him suddenly.

Our relationship is kind of strange right now. It's kind of screwy, him essentially being my boss during club business, but yet we're fucking. I cringe a little as I think of it. I can't believe this has even happened. Not just once, but it happened again today before I had planned to get out of bed.

We need to stop this until Avery is completely on board with it. But, at the same time, I want him any chance I get. I've always been the more dominant one, not taking any shit from people, but with him in control, I'll admit it's sexy as fuck. I still won't take no lip from anyone or anything, but if he wants to control me a little when we're alone, it gets my fucking dick hard seein' him like that.

This morning, Avery was asleep and he followed me in to the bathroom. He actually slept over from last night. Normally he doesn't stay, but I think he wants to give us that part of himself now; maybe he just wasn't ready before. I couldn't believe she hadn't heard us. He took me pretty roughly against the sink, the wall and cabinet creaking and groaning each time he slammed home. He felt so fuckin' amazin'. When we were finished, Avery was still sleeping. Her gorgeous auburn hair spread out over the pillow, with her hands tucked between her knees.

I haven't gotten up the nerve to say anything to her about it yet. What if she really isn't okay with wanting more than what we already have? Our whole relationship so far has been over being free and not tied down to any real serious shit. The most we've committed to each other is getting a pup and stayin' together here at the clubhouse, but it's come to the point where I want it all. Fuck, I have no clue what to even say at this point. All I know is I love her with every breath that I take; but now, I have all of these strong confusing feelings for Ares filling my head. I want everything, but I want it with both of them.

I don't know if I can say I'm really in love with Ares yet. The feelings for him are so different than what I feel for Avery. I feel this crazy need to protect her and cherish her. With Ares, I feel safe when I'm around him; I've been around him for years and trust him completely, even if I don't always act like it. He's smart and can take care of things, even more so now that he's the VP for the club, too.

I know he cares about Avery and me both, but does he love her like I do? Could he possibly love her the same way, so we can continue this...whatever this is? I couldn't handle it if he didn't have the same fierce need inside of him to protect her like I do, or the insatiable thoughts of having her all of the time.

She has the best pussy I've ever had in my life; but, at the same time, she has the sweetest fucking heart you could imagine. I'm ready to take the next step with her, and I fuckin' hope she's at that stage, too.

I started out with this whole threesome thing to bring Avery extra pleasure. The sharing never bothered me, because I know she loves me completely. I can't always give her everything she dreams of sexually, and Ares makes up for what I don't do. Is that how it's supposed to be? Is that why we all work so well together? *Fuck, I have to tell her about this.* I feel like scum, not being up front with her. I love her so much, and I know my heart will literally break if she's not okay with this.

Ares sits forward, drawing me out of my thoughts of Avery, resting his big, tattooed hands, full of silver chunky rings on the table close to mine. "I'm going to call the Prez and see what he thinks about this bullshit."

"What did the note even say?" I bite the inside of my cheek, curious.

"Some warped stupid shit about how the club has buried past VPs and to check our closets for skeletons, whatever the fuck that's supposed to mean." He shrugs.

"Buried VPs?" I repeat, squinting at him, puzzled.

"Yeah, I don't fuckin' know, brother. Your guess is as good as mine. The last VP was in an accident right around the time Prez got his patch, but I'm sure you're already aware of that. Anyhow, since then we haven't even discussed a new VP. Hell, I always believed it would be Smiles getting that spot if it ever came to it. Now, I get patched and this shit starts up. Fucked up bullshit drama is what it is."

"I just want to keep Avery safe this time; she's been hurt too many times already. I haven't let her leave the compound without me, and Cain's doin' the same with London. I have Sadie on lockdown unless it's for a doctor's trip and even then, myself or fuckin' Twist has to go. I hate it that she goes with him, but I know that crazy fucker will protect her ass and go off on anyone like a goddam rabid dog."

"Good, let's keep it that way. I don't want anything happening to any of you," Ares grumbles and taps his knuckles with mine easily. I leave my hand beside his, getting more comfortable with him being close.

"Hey boys, what are you two gabbing on about?" Pulling my hands back and resting them in my lap, Avery joins us at the table, sliding into the seat next to me.

I grunt and Ares replies with a grin, "Boys? Baby, I ain't no boy—all man right here." He winks at her and she returns it with her own mischief-filled grin. They've had a flirty, easygoing banter between them since they first met and there was a misunderstanding. Avery flipped out, thinking I was passing her off to Ares, not realizing we were both there to pleasure her together. Thankfully, they worked through it and became closer afterward.

Wrapping my arm around her, I tuck her small body close into my embrace in the booth. God, I fuckin' love her so much. With her and Ares both, life could be practically perfect. I don't know how long Ares is in this for or even if Avery will still love me after I confess to her what I want, but fuck, if they both stick around, my life would be completely full. Smiling down at her, I press a kiss on top of her head. Her hair always smells flowery and good. I love it that she's a girly girl; always busy paintin' her nails bright colors and shit. Crazy chick even painted Lily's nails when the poor pup was sleeping.

"Nothin' that concerns you, free bird." I murmur, breathing in her sweet smelling shampoo as I put my nose to her soft hair again. She probably thinks I'm a weirdo, always sniffing her, but damn, her hair smells nice. She's got lotion that smells so good, it makes me fuckin' hard as a rock, and her light smelling perfume she spritzes on every mornin', it's all got me addicted to seeing what she's put on when she's next to me. "What are you fixin' to do?"

"Well, I didn't see either one of you in the room after our fun night last night, so I figured I'd come looking for y'all and see if you wanted some lunch?"

"Hell yeah, shorty, if you're makin' lunch, I want some, please." I lean in, mumbling against her mouth and take her lips for a few seconds. Pulling back, I glance at Ares to see his eyes blazing, not in anger, but looking completely turned on, like he wants to be doing the same thing.

"Air?" Avery inquires and he blinks a few times.

"Sure angel, if you don't mind, I would love somethin.'"

She beams a large, happy smile at us, and jumps up and out of the booth., "Okay then, I'll be back!" She turns, strutting off, shaking her sexy ass in a little black pair of shorts as she heads for the kitchen. I can't help the pain in my gut, as the guilt for not being completely open with her hits me hard.

Facing Ares, I declare, "I'm telling her."

"The fuck you are. You wait."

"For what? She needs to know, any longer and she will never fuck-ing forgive me for not telling her sooner. I can't lose her, damn it. Ares, she means everything to me. I've never been this way over a woman before; you know how I was before she started staying here."

"You won't lose her. I told you already, I will take care of it."

"Yeah and how the fuck you gonna do that, huh?"

"Enough 2 Piece," he growls in warning. "Just calm your shit. I'll let you know when I speak with her. Everything will be motherfuckin' peachy."

Huffing, I cross my arms over my chest so I don't reach across the table and throat punch his ass. This is what he does to me—I either want him to fuck me or I want to kick him in the face.

I can't stand this. My heart hurts inside, imagining the possibility of losing her, of losing him, too. When did he become so important to me anyhow? We've been friends for years, but now what I feel for him is something completely different. Fuck if I'm not a little lost with it all. The same thoughts keep circulating over and over in my head. I feel like a damn pussy, whining and shit 'bout it all, but fuck.

"So the letter?" I move to distract myself with the issues at hand that can be easily fixed when I find the ignorant fucker who decided to grow a pair of balls during the night.

"I'm taking care of it," he shrugs.

"Don't keep me in the dark, damn it. Avery was fuckin' threatened, or did you forget? I want to know what's up."

He nods. "I know, and you will. You hear back from the last weapons' contact?"

"Yep, last night before you came to the room, and we're good with the Columbians, too. I don't know who the fuck would be threatening the club like this, let alone you."

"I don't know, either, but if shit doesn't fuckin' calm down soon, I may need to call Dom and get him here."

Dom was his friend he lived with before he joined the club. He's stopped in a few times and the brothers have met him. Dom seems much more normal than Ares, so he must have had a decent life growin' up. He rides a bike, but keeps his nose clean. We keep ours pretty clean also, but fuck knows we're all far from innocent.

We're interrupted by an out of breath Twist, as he comes rushing into the bar, scanning until he sees us. His long, blond hair is in every direction, as if he had just grabbed it and pulled it roughly.

"Fuck if Scratch didn't just see the same bike ride back by the club from the cameras!" Twist practically yells and Ares jumps up, anxious.

We have security cameras all over the compound to help us monitor if anyone comes and goes. Earlier when we left my room and got the note, we checked the footage. There was a white chopper with red skulls painted all over the tank. It was hard to make it out, but thankfully, Brently being a college brat, could figure out how to zoom in and out to see it better.

"Yo! They rode past the fuckin' compound?" Ares demands and Twist nods.

"Go see if you can catch him—only to town—and, if not, at least get me a fuckin' description!" Ares barks out, and Twist takes off running out of the club door.

"Fuck yeah! I'll be back," he cackles a crazed laugh, as the door slams closed.

"Should we call Cain?" I ask, standing beside him.

"No, they're at the ultrasound appointment. I'll text him in an hour to update him. Jamison was goin' to London's mom's house anyhow, so the boy is safe."

I nod, stirring through my thoughts, trying to figure out what else we should do. "Now what?"

"Now we wait and think." His hands flex, making tight fists as he takes his seat again.

"I fuckin' hate waitin'." I follow suit, sitting across from him.

"Fuck, I know, brother." He groans, shaking his head and pulls out his phone. Sitting quietly, I eavesdrop on his side of the conversation.

Spin?

Yeah, brother.

Just saw the chopper from last night. Keep your eyes peeled around the shop.

Naw, don't think they would. Just don't want you havin' any damages.

Yep, see ya then.

He hangs up, right as Avery breezes in, unaware of what just happened. She's carrying plates stacked with sub sandwiches and fruit salad. Ever since the BBQ last week, the brothers keep begging the girls to make London's mom's fruit salad. Fuck, that shit's hella good.

"Thanks, shorty." Murmuring, I take my plate from her, and she kisses me sweetly on the lips.

"Thanks, angel,' Ares nods, and she grins at him.

"No problem, now y'all dig in."

Avery has her own plate but she has a small sandwich and a heaping pile of fruit salad, pretty much the opposite of ours. We're all so hungry that we start shoveling in the delicious food.

After we're finished eating, I steal some of Avery's food, since she's been hoarding all of the fruit salad from us.

"If you will take the plates to the kitchen, I'm going to go call my dad." She stands, glancing between us.

"Yeah, of course. Thanks for makin' it."

"Welcome," she pops, kissing me tenderly on my cheek then rounds the booth, brushing a kiss on Ares' cheek as well. It doesn't upset me, though. If anything, it makes me happy to see her care for him, too. I guess maybe because I care for him a lot? Fuck knows.

I peer at him, questioningly.

"For fuck's sake, I told you, I'll take care of it. *Soon.*"

Nodding, I hold back. He better, I don't know if I can fucking wait any longer.

AVERY

the next morning

I'M AWOKEN BY STRONG FINGERS AND A LARGE, ROUGH PALM rubbing all over my naked flesh. His big, chunky silver rings are missing, having taken them off prior to lying down. The caresses feel so sweet; I burrow back towards it, to be met with an enormous, strong body. I can't believe it, but Ares actually stayed the whole night. He never stays, always dipping out, mumbling how he doesn't cuddle 'cause it's for pussies and he don't have one. This makes the second night now that he's stayed the entire time.

This morning I'm the lucky lady, lying completely exposed between these two incredible men. I have my gorgeous Silas, who's the love of my life on one side. Then I have Ares, who I'm quickly falling for, even though I know I shouldn't be, resting on the other side of me.

I try to keep my feelings in check, but it's so hard. I don't know if it's because I'm a woman and I get more emotionally attached, but it feels like Ares is a part of mine and 2 Piece's relationship. I don't know if that's good or if it's bad. I'm hoping it's a very good thing that I have feelings for him after what I heard in the bathroom yesterday morning. I don't know if they were both in there jacking off at the same time or if it there was more happening, but it was sexy as fuck. Once I heard the moaning, I couldn't help but reach inside of my panties to play with my clit, pleasuring myself to their sounds of ecstasy.

Then I pretended like I was asleep when they came out. I didn't want to embarrass them if they really were in there jacking off. Some men don't care, but others are weird about women knowing that they're handling their business. I've never heard of men doing it together in the same room though, so I'm thinking they were doing more. They could have easily woken me up, to join in with them if they wanted to have sex.

My thoughts are drawn away from yesterday, as Ares' hand slides over my tummy, pushing the sheet down as he goes. He heads straight to the bare juncture between my thighs. Adjusting my legs a little, I part them, giving him just enough room to slip a few thick fingers through my pussy lips and inside of me. As he pumps them inside a couple times, I coat his fingers in my wetness. My hips follow his fingers each time he tries to pull them free, craving more.

After a moment, he pulls his hand away, and I'm met with the warm, round tip of his cock, begging to enter me from behind. Adjusting more on to my side, I move so he can slip inside of me. He pushes in deeply on his first thrust.

Drawing in a heavy breath as he enters me, Ares stretches my pussy further to accommodate his size. My God, he feels so amazing. He rests his palm on my thigh, using it to help him tenderly drive into me.

Ares is being so soft and slow with me, the bed's barely even moving. 2 Piece snores away, unaware anything is happening. It's kind of an even greater turn on watching 2 Piece, knowing he's right in front of me as Ares is sliding inside.

I can't believe how freaking large he is, it brings a little pinch of pain each time he seats himself fully inside of me, feeling as if he's all the way into my stomach. He's never had his cock in my pussy before;

he's only ever taken my ass or my mouth. A completely new set of feelings explode through me, knowing that this is another step we're taking toward a point of no return.

His lips whisper over the delicate skin on my neck, bringing on an onslaught of chills, stimulating my body with each thrust, as his skilled mouth kisses me or his wet tongue caresses my ears, neck, and back.

My pussy pulses with each plunge, weeping in sweet pleasure and silently begging his cock for all it can give.

The sensations are beyond fantastic, having him taking me so gently, when he's only ever been rough with me. I feel cherished and loved, though I know I should only experience those kinds of feelings with 2 Piece.

Skirting his hand up my stomach he palms my small breast, occasionally tweaking my stiff nipple, and with each soft pinch, I bite my lips, barring down to keep me from calling out in ecstasy and to stop me from admitting my feelings to him out loud.

"I want you, angel," he murmurs, and my pussy clenches tightly around him in a frenzy at the sound of his rough voice.

"Hmm." I mumble quietly so he knows that I hear him, but also so I don't stir 2 Piece from his sleep.

Ares enters me again, running his fingertips over my skin until he cups my pussy, applying pressure to my clit with his palm.

Gasping out, I can't stop it; he hits the perfect spot everywhere. As he rubs his hand in slow circles, I feel like a huge tidal wave is coming for me.

"You need to be mine; you *both* need to be mine." He croons softly in my ear and at his words and the meaning behind them, I explode, my orgasm taking me so high I feel like I could float off of the bed.

He plunges into me powerfully as I ride through my orgasm. He sucks on the back of my neck as he seats himself fully, drawing my hip into him forcefully, filling me full of his seed.

After a moment, his taut body relaxes, and I feel his hot breath on the back of my neck as he pants. Ares tucks me into his body, wrapping me up in his arms, my body so small compared to his huge one. He doesn't squish me though. No, he holds me as if I mean the absolute world to him, and it's so precious to feel important.

The hard part is that it makes my feelings for him grow even deeper. I know I can't have two of them, but fuck if I don't want them both.

"You okay, angel? Did I hurt you?" he whispers.

Pulling myself free, I shift so that I'm facing him. He keeps his arm around me and I'm enveloped in his warmth. Peering into his dark irises, surrounded by thick lashes, I swear I see love shining in them. At least I pray that's what I really see and not just what I'm hoping to see.

Tenderly, I bring my small hand to his face, rubbing over his scruffy black trimmed beard; I can't help but smile at him. He leans into my touch, just like he always has, and I absolutely adore the fact I bring him some sort of comfort. I don't know what it is exactly, but I'm grateful it happens for him.

I can't believe this beautiful, caring man has a nickname like the butcher. People truly have no clue about him. I think he's misunderstood and deserves to be loved. What would 2 Piece say if he found out I'm falling in love with one of his brothers? Would he hate me, would they want to throw me out of the clubhouse? I'm so scared I could lose both of them.

Ares bends, until I'm close enough to lean up slightly and meet his mouth. His lips aren't thick, but just perfect enough so that when I kiss him, I feel as if I can't possibly get enough. He takes control of our kiss and I love every minute of it. He's still tender, enough so that I melt inside and if I were wearing any panties, they'd probably be on fire by now.

Pulling away slightly, I nod giving him a small smile. "I'm good, Air."

"Good. I mean it, angel; you're not just his, but mine, too."

"I can't talk about this right now." I whisper, my mind getting more confused and cloudy with what his words could mean.

He looks a bit unsure for a brief second, then his features smooth out, back to the confident Ares I'm accustomed to. "Okay, I'll give you a little time, but eventually, we'll discuss all this."

"Okay." I agree instantly, ready to move past the subject.

Ares kisses me softly one last time, pulling away and then he stands.

"Where are you going?"

"To my room."

"Because I won't discuss it all right now?"

"No, babe. 'Cause I need to take a shower and get shit done. 2 Piece needs to get some rest, so I'mma be quiet and bounce."

Biting my lip, I nod and scan over his face. I don't want things to get awkward just because I'm not ready to talk.

Ares gets his dark jeans and socks on, tucking his handful of rings into his front pocket. He holds his black leather biker boots and his T-shirt in one hand. His body casts the perfect shadows in the dawn light, accenting and highlighting his Spartan like muscles adorning his body. He could be one of the sculptures you see in a museum some-where, all smooth ridges and hard definition. His body may be mag-nificent, but I know that his heart is even greater.

"Ares," I call, carefully climbing from bed.

"Yeah, angel?" Pausing, his eyes glaze over with heat, as he watches my bare body come closer to him.

"Ares, are we good?" I repeat his own question, placing one hand on his tattooed chest and the other on his cheek. I have to know if this is going to be an issue. If so then we need to fix it before it gets worse. I can't handle not having him in my life like normal.

"Yeah, Avery, we're good, angel." He retorts sincerely and gives me a quick, chaste kiss on the lips.

I drop my hand as he pulls away. He gives me a soft, sated smile, which I answer with my own before he disappears out into the dark hallway, off to his own room, alone.

Closing the door quietly, locking it, I head to the bathroom. As much as I love Ares, I don't want his cum dripping down my legs when I go back to sleep next to Silas. I have to talk to him and tell him that I want them both. I just pray he understands that I'm still utterly in love with him and that it won't change, just because I need Ares, too.

three hours later...

I'm woken up to sloppy puppy kisses all over my face and Lily getting a mouthful of my hair, tugging until I shriek in pain. Freaking dog, she must need to go out. Peeling my tired eyes open, I glance around for 2 Piece, only he's nowhere in the room. It's silent, minus the dog, and smells strongly of his body spray. The guys must have had something happen for 2 Piece to not wake me up before he left the room.

Yawning, I sit up and pat Lily, while I attempt to pull on my grey yoga capris and a white tank top lying at the side of the bed. Fuck it, I'm in a biker club, no need for a bra this early. I doubt everyone will be up or here anyway. Most of the guys sleep until noon if they don't have to work. Only a few are early risers.

"Come on, girl." I stand, slipping my feet into my cheap plastic orange flip flops. Lily's either starving or has to pee. I'd rather attempt the outside trip first. I'd hate to be wrong and she pees on the floor in here. 2 Piece would probably flip out and rent a shampooer, cleaning the entire room and floor for just one little spot.

I help her into her black harness that's decorated with pink skulls and hook up the leash. We're training her to walk with it, so we started her out at a young age.

We make our way down the long hall and trek through the bar. Halfway through the room, I overhear a conversation I never thought I'd hear in a million years. Ares and 2 Piece are whisper shouting in a heated discussion and don't even notice us.

"Did you tell her yet?"

"No. I tried to early this mornin', but she wasn't ready to talk, brother."

"I told you, Ares, I have to be honest with her. I love her ass way too fuckin' much, man. She has to know 'bout us, or I can't keep doin' it."

"2 Piece, I told her I wanted ya' both. Give her a little time to think it over, for fuck's sake. Just calm your shit."

I hurry Lily along, not wanting to hear any more of a conversation that they think is private. Clearly, it sounds like 2 Piece won't have an issue when we *do* finally talk about it. It sounds as if we each want the same things together, but we're afraid of what the other will say. We have to fix this and soon.

We make our way out of the enormous metal back door, where Lily usually goes to the bathroom.

I can't believe what I just overheard. That's freaking crazy. Ares and 2 Piece? What does that even mean? Have they been seeing each other without me? Is that what was going on in the bathroom? It hurts to know they haven't told me about it, but I have to admit it really turned me on yesterday imagining them together like that. It would mean that I could have them both. *Fuck!*

We make it out into the grassy area. Lily runs ahead, excited as usual. I'm lost in my own thoughts of how everything is going to play out or what could possibly happen. I'm caught off guard as Lily starts growling a low rumble of warning; she's been slowly learning to growl from when she plays with the guys. Ares has been working on some sort of training methods with her when he has her, and she's been learning all kinds of new stuff.

Her short black hair fluffs up along her spine as she starts to bark. She's never alerted me to anything before, and I get spooked and quickly glance up.

I'm met with the creepy green eyes from the same scary-looking man I saw at the grocery store standing about twenty feet away from me. This time, however, he's not alone, but accompanied by another stringy-haired guy. Wearing sinister grins, they both appear extremely pleased that they've caught me outside alone. The only thing I can think of is to scream bloody fucking murder and hope someone hears me. My body crawls with the thoughts of what they may do to me if they catch me.

"ZZZZZZZZZZZZZZZZZZZZ!" I bellow frantically and hastily follow up with, "Areeeeeeeeeees! Hellllp!" I wring my hands together, clenching them into tight fists as my voice hits a pitch I didn't know it was capable of. My nails digging into my palms reminds me that my ass needs to run and get the hell away *now*.

Lily's leash drops to the ground as my heart starts to beat wildly, full of a fresh dose of adrenaline. My sandals slide a little as I take off running, pumping my legs toward the back door as fast as I possibly can. If they want me, then they're going to have to catch me first, and then I'll fight them with every last breath I have in my body. Ares' proud expression from the church meeting the other day flashes through my mind, and I promise myself that I'll have him gaze at me like that again. I won't give in to these rat bastards.

These men are not here to be my friend, but to hurt me...especially after London clipped the one dark-haired guy with Cain's car. I hear Lily start snarling and barking like she's a grown watchdog, and I've never been prouder. "Lily! Come!" I shout behind me as I sprint the distance back towards the club door, pumping my arms wildly. Fuck, we're never going that far away into the yard again.

The club's back door crashes open, making a loud clapping sound as it hits the wall behind it. Ares comes thundering through it at full speed, his powerful thighs on a mission as they pound over the ground toward me. 2 Piece and Brently hurriedly come running right behind him. Ares looks absolutely murderous when he sees the guys trying to get to me.

2 Piece has one of his Glocks out already. He quickly rushes to me, tucking me behind him. "The fuck you doin' out here?"

"Just walking the dog," I squeak, but he doesn't respond. He keeps his gun trained toward Ares and Brently as they charge the two creeps. If Ares or Brently get hurt, then 2 Piece will start shooting. I'm honestly surprised he hasn't just shot and killed both of them already.

Lily runs toward me, spooked. She freaked out when the two guys ran past her. She was still in her spot holding strong, barking her little head off; I guess until she knew we were safe.. I squat down to pick her up and wrap her in my arms as soon as she gets close enough to me. Just a puppy and yet already standing up to protect me. What a good freaking dog. "It's okay, Lily, you're such a good girl."

I watch as everything unfolds; it all happens as if in slow motion.

ARES

As soon as I heard the screech coming from out back, I knew something was off. The first thing that came to mind was that Avery was alone and unprotected. Thank fuck it's morning; if the music or TV had been playing, we'd have never heard her.

When I open the back door and see them, I start to run for her. The way the pup was growling and barking, I knew right away that those men intended to harm Avery. Not the bitch I love...I don't fucking think so.

I push my legs as hard as possible, driving them to charge at the fuck sticks, full speed. Throwing my fist out, I catch one of them in the shoulder with enough of an impact he stumbles back a few steps before regaining his balance.

The other steps towards me and I punch him directly in the throat. He keels over right as Brently catches up. The guy's bent over, gasping for air, and Brently starts wailing all over the dude's head and back. Fuck it, whatever works I guess.

This little slimy fuck matches the description of the white bike Twist gave me yesterday after he was able to catch the tail end on him. The guy steps toward me, and I raise my foot, sending a swift kick to the guy's stomach.

"Who the fuck are you," I bellow.

"Fuck you," he spits out and comes at me again. He punches me in my stomach, but it doesn't faze me. I've been doing this shit for way too long to have one hit be able to fuck me up.

"My turn motherfucker," I growl.

Latching onto each of his ears with my hands, I bring his head to mine, head-butting him in the nose. He goes down quickly, blood oozing out of his nose, going everywhere. The moment he hits the dirt I give him a few swift, hard kicks in the ribs. It's enough that I know a few are cracked if not broken. It'll at least slow him down enough so that I can get him to the shed and tied up.

I'mma saw this motherfucker into tiny pieces, then feed him to the pigs at the farm. Thinkin' he can come around here, fucking with my family, with my fucking club. No way, not fucking happening.

His gun peeks out of the back of his pants, so I swiftly snatch it up and tuck it into my own pants. Glancing over to Brently, I find that he's kicking the other guy all to hell. The guy's face is completely covered in blood. Hell, at this point, I don't know if he's even alive anymore. Brother has a lot of anger trapped inside of him after all that Twisted Snake MC bullshit went down. I still can't get over how they carved Brently's stomach up, threatening the club president's son with gutting him. Fucking people never learn.

"Yo, Brently, stop brotha' we need 'em alive so I can fuck with 'em for information. Gripping his arm tightly, I wrench him away from the guy on the ground. He's unmoving, so he's not going anywhere. Brently turns, ready to strike at me, but I catch his arm before he can. "Pull yourself together!"

He nods, swallowing. He takes a step back and pulls on his bloody shirt in an attempt to straighten it. Yeah, like that will fix that shit. I learned many years ago to always wear black. Those white shirts are good for nothing, they just get greasy or bloody in this way of life.

Twist comes walking around the corner, eyes widening in alarm and then to excitement when he sees what's going on.

"Twist, go get me some rope."

"All right." He takes off to the shed.

The guy at my feet lets loose a painful groan.

"Trust me, it may feel like it hurts now, but you ain't got no fuckin' idea what I plan to do to you. Just wait. You'll learn a whole new meanin' of pain by the time I'm done with ya."

ARES

a couple of hours later

BRUSHING A FEW WAYWARD STRANDS OF HAIR OUT OF MY eyes, I take stock of the two pieces of shits we have tied up in the shed. They didn't fight much. Hell, they didn't even move much.

I rang the Prez straight away but he said Mona's having too bad a day for him to leave her. I was surprised, since he's been itching to hear about what these guys know and want. I'm curious myself on what they'll have to say. I understand him putting her first though; he never used to and it's 'bout time he did.

"Errmmm," The dickface guy who threatened Avery moans out.

"Shut the fuck up," Twist snarls, popping the guy on the side of the head. He approaches the other guy that Brently was laying into, kicking at his legs. "You alive, pussy?"

The man doesn't respond and Twist shrugs. He steps away from him and pulls out his grey case filled with his special set of knives he had tucked in his back pocket. Unrolling the convenient pouch, he selects a medium-sized, serrated blade. Inspecting the shiny blade, he nods, carefully placing the pouch on the bench nearby. The teeth on that blade would hurt like hell, doing some serious damage to its intended target.

"This should work nicely," Twist says aloud to no one in general. "Let's see just how dead you really are, stupid fucker."

With that he crouches down in front of the tied-up guy, slitting the man's right pant leg from shoe to knee. Twist carefully folds the damaged jeans away, exposing the unconscious man's skin on his lower leg.

His face lights up, almost as if he were just presented with a prize as he gazes on the bared flesh. Kissing the side of the blade closest to him, Twist whispers to himself cryptically, "I still hear you." I've heard him murmur this on multiple occasions when he plays with his knives. With that, he drives the blade forcefully into the fleshy part beside the man's shin. The guy remains still and Twist glares, irritated he didn't make him cry out or get *any* response from him.

He shakes his head, mumbling to himself and slits the pant leg up higher, producing the man's thigh. Twist chuckles lowly, tossing the blade to catch it in his left hand. Before I even blink he drives it quickly into the meaty area closest to the man's cock. *Still nothing.* Twist growls low in his throat in response.

Time to interrupt before Twist goes on a stabbing spree and riddles the guy full of stab holes. "Look Brother, I think Brently put the motherfucker in a coma or some shit. He hasn't moved since I pulled the brother off of him. He's barely even breathing, so fuck knows."

He nods, gesturing to my next victim. "Can I have him then?"

"No. He will be dealt with by me."

"You sure 'bout that, Ares? I've got plenty more knives I could use on him; we could have some fun."

"How 'bout you go ask 2 Piece to come on out here for a sec."

"Oh, I'm the fuckin' gopher boy now?"

Growling, I glare, "Seriously, Twist?"

"I'll be back." He grins. Twist is always trying to stir shit up for whatever reason.

Once I have a few of my saws plugged in, I scoot them closer to the idiots. I unfold a large sheet of black painters' plastic around the dark-haired asshole's chair. I grab my black rubber butcher's apron, tying it snuggly to help keep the blood off my clothes. Not that it really matters about it staining, being that I'm dressed in all black attire, but I sure hate the fucking smell. That weird scent and copper like taste when it sprays on your lips and you lick them, forgetting about it. I don't mind the warm blood on my hands; it's cathartic, renewing the memory of bathing my skin in my father's blood. The crimson liquid is there coating my skin with each kill, to remind me that I overcame an extent of evil and prevailed.

"What's your name?"

"Ermmmm."

"You need to tell me your fuckin' name, this shit won't fly with me motherfucker."

He stays silent and I huff. They always try to hold out, stupid idiots. He probably won't even make it to his small ass wrist before he gives in. They never do, bunch of goddamn pansy asses.

"I'mma call you screamer, 'cause I bet you're a bigger bitch than you lead on."

Circling Screamer's plain, sturdy metal chair, I grip the back piece behind his shoulders and pull him a little closer to my saw. Grabbing the roll of trash bags off the bench, I place a few underneath him around the chair. I don't need to make a mess. The painter's plastic will help keep it off the ground but all of the body parts need to go somewhere or the blood will bleed through any hole it can find. I've learned a lot since my bleach scrubbing days as a kid.

It's easier to just burn the nasty smelling plastic, then bury the remaining melted pieces, effectively getting rid of the blood evidence. Now if it's a whole body, I'll usually dump the blood back in the river close by. Don't need no fuckin' coppers snooping around looking for anything. In this case, I'm gonna bag up all of the body parts and take 'em out to feed the pigs at the farm close by. It's been awhile since I was out toward that way, and I know they enjoy a special treat occasionally.

Light floods in to the room as Twist opens the door again, returning with 2 Piece. As soon as 2 Piece notices the dark-haired man, he launches himself at him, ready to rip the scum apart. Twist leaps toward 2 Piece before he can get to the chair, tugging an irate 2 Piece away, keeping him close to the door.

Twist gawks at me, flustered, attempting to hold on, "Ares, you wanna hurry it the fuck along, brother? 2 Piece isn't the easiest to hold when he's pissed."

"2 Piece, calm down, for fuck's sake. I gotta ask him a few things, then you can have him."

His eyes flair as he snarls, "Let me ask the motherfucker some questions!"

"Not yet, can you chill the fuck out so Twist can let you go?" 2 Piece nods briefly and Twist releases him. 2 Piece shoves Twist away a few feet, irritated that he was holding him and Twist snickers, fully amused. "Don't start, either one of y'all. I get you're fuckin' heated 2 Piece, but let me find out what I can first."

"Then I can do what the fuck I want with him?"

"Yeah, man." I'm surprised he even decided to ask; normally this sort of thing makes him way too queasy. I get it, though. It's personal when it comes to a threat toward Avery. I wanted to have a few witnesses if these dicks decide to talk, especially to make sure all of the facts make it back to Prez. "Where's Cain?"

2 Piece glares at me growling, "Sitting with the girls. He wanted to come, but they begged him to stay if I had to go."

Sighing, I nod. Cain should be doing this shit, technically being the Enforcer and all, but I know he probably wants to stay with London to make sure she's alright emotionally and remains safe. He's been stuck to her like glue ever since she admitted to being pregnant. I get that, but the brother just got his fuckin' patch as Enforcer, and as VP, I shouldn't be getting' so dirty anymore. Everybody's either thirstin' for blood or fuckin' dippin' out of their shit they need to handle.

The shed door creaks as it opens again and more light pours in "This where the party's at?" Spin cheekily inquires and 2 Piece grunts.

"Any more of y'all gonna come triapsin' through the fuckin' door before I get anywhere?" I grumble as I start to picture how it's going to feel when my saw blade begins to grind through this asshole's bones. I may let 2 Piece play with him, but in the end I will be the one wearing his blood.

"Naw man, but I can go get some pom poms and shit if you'd like? What color?" Spin snickers.

Shaking my head, I smirk, "Get yourself a fuckin' skirt while you're at it, bet it'd fit your ass perfect."

"Ermmm," Our heads all quickly turn toward Screamer as he moans. He's probably hurting; I got a good one to his jaw, pretty sure that's fuckin' broken now.

"Hey ya, Ares, let me carve him up some, yeah?" Twist asks with an almost childlike excitement.

I sigh loudly and shake my head. "Screamer, you gonna talk yet?"

"Ummph."

Rubbing my hands together, I smile for the first time since I was lying in bed with Avery. I step next to him and my saw, untying his left hand; I bring it next to my miter saw. I line up his dirty, weathered palm right where my blade will slice off from his knuckles on up. It's easier for the pigs to eat it in smaller pieces anyhow.

"Oh fuck, I can't watch this shit," 2 Piece says and turns so his back is facing me. Twist and Spin chuckle as the room echoes with the shrill ringing sound of my saw.

I hold the handle tightly with my left hand and the Screamers arm with my right, applying pressure. The blade lowers and starts to make a grinding sound, almost sounding as if it's choking as it tears through the thin meat into the muscle of the hand. Blood spatters all over me, and I keep smiling, as I reminisce with the feelings washing through my system. The saw smokes and a strong fleshy smell bathes the room as it finally cuts the body parts completely off.

As the saw silences, the echoes of screaming meets my ears and suddenly I possess Screamer's full attention.

"Ah, there you are fuckface. Told ya you'd fuckin' scream with the first one, huh? Glad your bitch ass didn't pass out. Now shut the fuck up, and tell me why you came after my chick?" The words leave my mouth without me realizing what I've even said. The brothers remain silent. 2 Piece knows the seriousness of my declaration in front of club members, but the other brothers, I'm sure, believe it's just an angle I'm using to get some information.

"Please, please, please."

"You can beg as much as you want. This is what I do. I can chop you up, piece by motherfucking piece, until you tell me what I want to know."

"Okay, okay!" He cries, clear snot dripping from his crooked nose as he pleads. "I-I," he takes a deep, broken breath "Your Prez had a deal, and he broke it."

"A deal? What kind of a deal, and how the fuck does it affect my club?"

"Yes...he wasn't supposed to get another VP. We heard that your club patched in someone for the spot."

"Yep...and? The fuck we supposed to do, never have another VP? Get the fuck outta here."

"Yes." He coughs, clearing phlegm. "No VP for as long as your Prez is alive."

"What the fuck for? What did he get out of this shit?"

"He became President."

The room silences completely as the weight of his words shower over each of us, and our minds race with this type of implication. Either we just found out a huge chunk of secret information the Prez has been keepin' for a hell of a long time, or this cock sucker is begging for a miserable death.

"You realize what the hell will happen to you if this is all a fuckin' lie?"

"Please, yes man! Shit, my hands already no good now; I ain't got no reason to lie to any of you. You think I'd break into a motorcycle compound just for shits and giggles. Fuck! I'm only following orders!"

I glance over at Twist, 2 Piece, and Spin. I'm so conflicted on what the fuck to do at this point. I definitely need more information, but fuck me, if this is true. The guy starts to sweat profusely, shaking and pale. He could go into shock, and that's the last thing I need to deal with right now. I grab an old greasy shop rag and throw it at him, then untie his other hand so he can hold the cloth tightly to his wound. His legs are still tied, so he can't go anywhere. Not that I'm worried about him getting away. I'd just catch his ass again and maybe cut a foot off next time.

"Now why couldn't he have a new VP, and who are you exactly?"

"I'm just a messenger; this came from my uncle and his club."

"Tell me why can't we have another VP?"

"I was told your President struck a deal with my uncle. My uncle's brother was supposed to be next at your table to be in line for President."

"You mean the old VP that died?"

"Died?" He looks at me incredulously. "No, he was brutally murder-ed, so your President could have his spot instead. My uncle warned him that he would kill every VP your club patches until your President, now, finally dies."

"Well, that's fuckin' dumb."

The man shrugs, breathing deep raged breaths, clearly in a lot of pain.

"Grow some fuckin' balls and man up; I've seen men make it to the wrist before they act like a goddamn vagina about it." I grumble and turn to my brothers.

The man surprisingly pales further at my words. I didn't think that was possible. Apparently he thought I was only gonna chop a few fingers up.

"Well?" I question my brothers. I definitely need their input on this shit here.

Twist, 2 Piece, and Spin gawk at me, looking angry and confused.

2 Piece hisses, "I still get my turn with him," and gestures towards Screamer.

"In time, brother. First we need to speak with the others about this, and then we need to talk to Prez." They all chin lift and I secure Screamer's hands again. "Oh, and what's your fuckin' name?"

"Jake, man, my name is Jake."

Nodding, we all head to the door; I lock up the shed and follow my brothers inside the clubhouse. This is going to be one nasty cluster-fuck. I already know the brothers are gonna go berserk if all this shit Jake's been spouting out is really true.

We hit the bar up first and I go straight for the whiskey, 'cause fuck this sober shit. Prez is the closest damn thing I have had to a father figure. Hell, he's the closest to just a plain old family member in general. I'm gonna have to call church without him knowin' about it, and that drives me crazy inside. Should I speak to Smiles privately and try to learn what he knows, or just have it out in front of all of the brothers?

No, there are clearly way too many secrets as it is. I'm gonna have everyone in on this, so shit doesn't get screwed up. Shooting down the remainder of whiskey left, I slam my glass down, angry. I can't believe I'm the one fuckin' dealin' with this shit. I just got my goddamn patch.

A small hand lands on the center of my back and I turn, finding Avery's worried honey colored gaze. "Yo, angel. Not a good time, beautiful."

"Are you all right? You slammed that glass down on the counter so hard, I was surprised it didn't shatter everywhere." Her worried honey irises flicker all over my face, coming to meet my dark gaze again.

"I'll be straight wit' ya'. Right now you should be with 2 Piece." Swallowing, she peers up at me, lookin' hurt that I'm chasing her off, but I need to think about this shit. There's too much going on, and I have too many responsibilities in all of it. It's gonna fall on me to make sure it all gets handled the way it's supposed to.

This is why we're all so perfect together as a unit. 2 Piece can give her this kind of attention she needs. Me, on the other hand, I'm colder inside. I'm not good at all that comforting and lovey-dovey bullshit. I lie to myself, pretending that her touch doesn't calm my racing heart, that it doesn't bring me renewed hope in having someone in my life. It does though. It makes me want to be better, for her and for myself. 2 Piece will take me like this, but I need to learn to be a little softer for Avery.

She leans in, kissing me softly on the bottom of my jaw and then walks away, giving me exactly what I just requested. She does it without asking me any questions about it at all, and I think my heart just completely went with her.

"Church!" I bellow loudly and the brothers whip their heads toward me. "Now." I grunt and gesture to the Chapel. They all set their drinks down immediately, making their way into the room. We're missing a few people, but there are enough here to discuss the issue at hand. I don't think I can wait anyhow. I'm brimming over inside with anger and deceit. I need to get to the bottom of this shit that could possibly break the fuckin' club in half.

Church...

I take my seat and everyone stares at the Prez's seat. Well, all of them but Twist, 2 Piece, and Spin, that is.

"We have a problem to discuss." I glance around at everyone's faces. "Prez ain't here, and it's too important to wait on it." Smiles peers at me puzzled, and I decide to get started with him.

"Smiles, brother, do ya know anything about what happened to the last VP of this club?"

"Yep, he got into a wreck and passed on. God rest his soul."

"We all know that story. I'm talkin' 'bout what the fuck else happened to him?"

He shrugs, suspiciously glaring at me.

Nightmare grunts, "Ares, wanna clue us the fuck in? I ain't got time for no fuckin' guessin' games, you feel me, brah?"

Shifting my glare to him, I huff. I think he and Exterminator are decent people, we've been cool for a while, but interrupting me is a fuckin' no go. I may be the VP and not the Prez, but right now I'm highest other fucker at the table, and he needs to shut the fuck up 'till I'm done.

"Pretty sure I was getting to it brother, wanna fuckin' cookie while you wait?" I growl in response, and he grins. "Now, before I was fuckin' interrupted, there was some shit I was heading toward. Does anyone know of a different story about what happened to the last VP?"

The room stays silent, and I flex my hands into tight fists. For fuck's sake, I can't believe I'm put in this fucking position right now. It boils my blood inside.

I crack my knuckles and rehash what Jake admitted to us in the shed. The brothers all react the same way 2 Piece, Twist, Spin, and I had—with anger, hurt, confusion, and skepticism. All of them except for Smiles. He wears a smirk like he's pleased it finally came out.

Cocking my eyebrow, I confront him, "Well?"

"Nah, let Prez tell you 'bout it. This ain't my shit to share."

ARES

CHURCH ENDS WITH A GROUP OF PISSED OFF BROTHER WHO head back out to the bar. I'm about to head to my booth when I overhear 2 Piece runnin' his fuckin' mouth off to Exterminator, and it's pretty much my breaking point after all the shit going down today. First Avery being attacked, then this crap about Prez, and now him.

"I'm serious, he's the fuckin' Butcher for God's sake, and everyone knows it. He should have diced that piece of shit up already. No, instead he's busy fuckin' around with this Prez bullshit playing goddamn detective. I mean if he can't do his shit, maybe I should be allowed to take care of it."

Fuming inside, I bellow loudly, "2!"

Turning towards me, he cocks an eyebrow, "Yeah?"

"You think I don't hear you motherfucker? Been real fuckin' tired of your bullshit here lately."

"And? You know Avery deserves justice, yet you sit in here, fretting like a fucking cow."

"Get to your room so we can talk 'bout this shit."

"Why the fuck can't we talk about it here?" He widens his arms, gesturing to the bar littered with club members.

"You really wanna hash our shit out in front of everyone? I don't give a flyin' fuck, brother; we can do this shit here."

He huffs, storming off down the hallway to his room, clearly pissed off that I had called him out on it.

The room's fairly quiet after he leaves, and everyone's staring at me. "The fuck? I'm the motherfucking Butcher, aye? Move the fuck on, unless you wanna find out how I got my fuckin' name," I grit out and head toward 2 Piece's room after him.

Catching 2 Piece at the door, I grasp onto his shoulder, holding him in place and ripping the door open. I propel him into the room. Slamming the door and heaving him up against it. "The motherfucking Butcher, huh?" I hiss, close to his face. "You up for gossiping like a little bitch when you don't get your way? Don't get it fuckin' twisted. Just 'cause we're fuckin' don't mean I won't handle my shit with you in front of the fuckin' brothers. Disrespect me again motherfucker."

He smacks his palms against my chest, heatedly, growling, "Well, what the fuck? I thought you cared about Avery? I thought you fucking cared about me? That shit was different, yet you're not giving me the justice I crave, the justice I fucking deserve! Did you see her face after she was basically attacked? You didn't ride with her the last time she was shot! You haven't a fucking clue, and you wanna call me out? I'll run my mouth if you fuckin' deserve to hear it!"

"You brother, have no goddamn idea how much I care for her or for you! I know you deserve justice, and you will fucking have it."

"You care, huh? Oh, I'll fucking believe it when I see it!" He shouts, and I can't control myself.

Thrusting my body against his, my lips hover over his as I hiss, "Yes, I fucking care! I fucking love her for fuck's sake, and not just her you idiot, but you as well!"

As the words come tumbling out, 2 Piece perks up, bends forward and takes my mouth in haste. His hands trail up my chest, wrap behind my neck and pull me closer to him, as I grip onto his hips. Driving my pelvis into him, my cock goes ramrod stiff and I grind into him, finding his own hardness through his jeans. Feeling my cock rub against his, fully clothed is a turn on like no other.

I pull my mouth away on a gasp, as he moans, "I fucking love you, too, Ares, both of you, I just love both of you."

Leaning in, I take his mouth again, ripping his shirt up and over his head quickly, seeking his nakedness, wanting to take him, to own him completely. 2 Piece scrambles, rushing to pull my shirt off of me and unbutton my pants. God, I fucking love him and his impatience. Drawing him away from the wall, I shift our bodies so I can walk him to the bed, while I glance over his shoulder, making sure we can make it without falling.

I'm not met with the bed, however. Instead, I'm met with a warm set of honey colored eyes, overflowing with heat. She's been in here the entire time. She fucking heard all of it. I stop completely, and 2 Piece's eyes shoot open, questioning me. Staying silent, I nod behind him to the bed.

His forehead wrinkles slightly, and he turns, glancing back to the bed. A gasp of her name trembles off his lips in shock, as he finally comes face-to-face with Avery, and our secret is wide out in to the open.

"Sh-Shorty, please, I can explain."

Avery's gaze shifts between him and me, squinting, "Explain what, Silas? I think it's pretty clear."

"Fuck, free bird, please don't hate me. I love you so much; I don't want to hurt you. Fuck, I'm such a fuck up. Always screwing shit up with you." He shakes his head, upset.

"Hate you? No Silas, I love you, very much, in fact. I was battling my feelings inside this whole time, because I actually love you both." She finishes on a whisper and my throat hurts hearing about her feelings. Knowing that she loves me, too, right after 2 Piece had finally admitted how he really feels.

I don't know why my throat hurts and it feels like I can't swallow, but after a moment the feeling dissipates, calming down, and I take a relaxing breath for the first time all day.

His eyes grow wide. "You serious 'bout that right now, Avery Marie? I know I keep screwin' this shit up. I'm sorry, I keep tryin' to do right by you, I swear to fuckin' God. I don't wanna fuck it all up with you."

She nods, bending her head to look at the bed. "I'm completely serious, Silas. We still need to talk about everything though, about how this will work, but I want you both." She picks her head back up, peering at me, "That is, if you'll have me." I swallow harshly at her confession, wanting to charge her and rain kisses all over her body.

"Oh, thank God. I had no fuckin' clue how to tell you 'bout this an' all. I love you so fuckin' much free bird. I'm really sorry; I promise you mean the fuckin' world to me." 2 Piece rushes to Avery's side of the bed, sitting beside her, looking worried. Avery pulls him to her quickly, kissing him wildly to get him to stop his pleading and apologizing. He lovingly holds her face in his palms, studying her, making sure she's okay. After a few moments, she pulls away, stands up from the bed and makes her way in front of me.

Staring up to me with her sweet-as-sin eyes, she licks her lips and lightly wraps one of her fingers around my pinky. The gentleness she always shows me makes my heart swell, and I lean down, wrapping my arm around her small waist. I lift up her petite body, bring her close and hold her tightly as she's finally at my level.

Murmuring, I put myself and my feelings out on the line to her, "Angel, I *will* keep you, if you let me."

Her face lights up and she comes closer, bumping my nose lightly with her own. "I love you, Air."

"And I love you, Angel." Her saying those words makes my heart swell so much; it feels as if it may burst. Who would think that a few words would make such a difference when you finally hear them from the woman you adore? The thing with Avery is that I know I won't have to worry about her running off with some fucking Mexican biker gang like my ex. She has 2 Piece and me both, I actually trust her. 2

104

Piece is the same, he may drive me to fuckin' madness with his smart ass mouth sometime, but in the end, I know I can trust him and that I love him.

I'm confident that by the way they both look at me, that they love me. The rest of the world matters even less, knowing I have them both. Our relationship may not be what is known as normal, but it's what works for us.

We're interrupted by a knock on the door, and I automatically open the door widely, still holding Avery close to my chest.

Spins big ass black Mohawk and freaky colored eyes greet me, "Yo?" I grumble, wanting to get back to my previous conversation.

"Hey man, Prez is on the compound. The fuck you gonna do about that bull from earlier?"

"Shit, of course this pops off when I'm in the middle of somethin' important."

Avery places her soft hand on my cheek, instantly consuming the bulk of my attention. "Go take care of things, I won't be going anywhere, I promise." I nod, placing a chaste kiss on her lips, setting her back down and catching Spin peering into the room at a shirtless 2 Piece sitting on the bed.

"Can I help you, brother?" Grumbling, I pull my shirt back on.

Blinking, Spin meets my dark gaze. "Nope.. Just happy for you man."

"Quit being sappy an' shit, let's go."

Spin grins cheekily and heads back toward the bar. I pop back in the door, "Brother?" 2 Piece looks up, "Church, you comin'?" He nods and I make the trek to the bar.

Time to figure some shit out.

twenty minutes later in church again...

Prez scans the room, taking in all of the brothers' angry faces until he lands on mine, puzzled. "The fuck's goin' on VP? What's this I hear, I missed church? I didn't get a fuckin' notification I was needed."

Clenching my jaw, my mind races on what to say and how to go about it all, no way will probably be the right way in the end. It's times like these, that fuckin' suck being in this position, it would be entirely too easy if this responsibility fell to another's shoulders. However, my life has never been an easy one.

"Yeah, your right, it's because you weren't invited."

"Excuse the fuck outta me? The fuck you just say to me, boy?"

"I'm no boy, old man, I've told you this. It has been brought to our attention you may have wronged the club, and we had to discuss what was the best thing to do about it."

"I've wronged the club? Have you fuckin' lost it? I love *my* club. Who the fuck are you exactly, to question me?"

"This is our club also, and it's my job as VP to protect it. When I was speaking to Avery and London's attacker, some information about the club was brought to our attention."

"Who the fuck was the guy and what did he say?"

"Well, how about we start with you tellin' us all what happened to the last VP."

"Last time I checked, you don't fuckin' give me orders. Now tell me what the fuck was said!"

Cain stands suddenly, his chair flying backward from the impact and bellowing angrily, "Enough bullshit! I'm the fucking Enforcer of this club now. Prez, tell us what the fuck happened, then Ares can tell you what we found out and we can compare stories. I'm sick of this back and forth shit; you're both just wasting fucking time while we have shit to get taken care of." He turns, scooting his chair back and sitting. Once he's settled, he folds his arms over his chest and cocks his eyebrow, clearly waiting on us to follow orders.

We all stare at him, taken aback by his outburst. I'm pretty proud of him right now; he did exactly what the Enforcer *should* do when there is an issue like this. He thought of what's best for the club at the moment, not about who he would end up pissing off. Clearing my throat, I nod and give my attention to Prez.

Prez takes a swallow of his bottled water and leans forward to spill his story. "It's complicated and it's my fuckin' business, not y'alls', but I'll tell ya, just to nip this shit in the ass right away. This dates back to before any of you were here, well except Smiles," he glances briefly at Smiles. Not angrily, but in defeat.

"I may have made a few mistakes back then, but I was a man and had to deal with shit the way I saw fit." He looks between Cain and me, "Ares, Cain, the reason why I showed you where I kept important documents and told you to protect them is because they contain some proof on a crime I committed many years ago."

Taking a calming breath, he focuses back on all of the brothers. "This club used to be about three of us really—myself, Smiles, and another brother, Max. We were all close, growing up together and eventually getting into motorcycles. Hell, we did everything with each other. They were my best friends, my brothers, and I trusted them completely. We were into a bunch of shit, running a bunch of drugs, partying with different one percenter clubs, shit was different back then. We were different ourselves, I think we were all sampling way too many drugs and shit wasn't so cut-and-dried, like now." Smiles nods, a far-off look on his face as he remembers.

The room is eerily silent as we all impatiently wait to hear the rest. No one's smoking, drinking, or taking their eyes from Prez and Smiles. We want to hear all of it.

"Most of y'all ain't real familiar with my Mona. Boy she was the fuckin' cat's meow back then." His eyes glaze a little and a small grin tilts the corner of his mouth as he thinks of her. "Long, straight platinum blonde hair brushing the top of her plump ass, rich chocolate brown eyes with a set of tits that would make you fuckin' cream your pants, and she was all mine. Smiles was with her sister, Veronica, and Max was with one of their girlfriends named Rachel." Prez shakes his head as Smiles appears heartbroken when he hears Veronica's name being mentioned.

"Y'all know how club life is; none of us had any idea about the ride we were in for. Max had an older brother that was in a ruthless one percenter club, called the Iron Fists."

A few small inhales are heard as brothers draw in deep breaths at the name of one of the most notorious motorcycle clubs known in the United States. They were full of ruthless men, feared by bikers everywhere for a time. They aren't quite as known now, after keeping their heads down. Many court appearances and federal cases got them to do their dirty work on the down low versus wide out in the open like they used to.

"Well we started hanging around them, thinkin' 'bout prospectin' for 'em and ended up partyin' a little too hard. Regular drug use got us all pretty strung out. None of us were expecting to have the women flocking to us, wanting to be associated with the club. Being around them, their ways started rubbing off on us."

Prez runs his hands over his face, looking stressed. "Max started beating his Ol' Lady, Rachel, and I started fuckin' random club snatch. Fuck knows why, Mona was fucking perfect compared to all of 'em. We were just fuckin' dumb I 'spose. We weren't worrying about the consequences, about treating our women like shit and getting fucked up all the time. Mona got sick of me runnin' around on her and started to eat up the attention Max was givin' her. Max and Mona were always good friends, had been since we were all in high school together, so I didn't think much of it at the time." I light a cigarette, inhaling deeply, because fuck if I don't know where this is headed.

"Smiles started working on getting us clean, volunteering our small group to go on long runs with the guys. They all still partied and had women on the runs, but it was extremely low-key compared to what went down at the clubhouse. I started to see what was happening the cleaner I got, and I helped Smiles try to get us all off of the drugs and away from the club."

He takes a long drink from his bottled water. "By the time I realized what was going on with Mona, it was too late. I was completely sober when I caught her and Max. She had gotten tired of waiting, of loving me while I did whatever the fuck I wanted with whomever I saw fit. She eventually succumbed to Max and had a fling with him. I caught them and threatened Max to back off or I'd kill 'im. We grew apart, and Mona and I were having major fights. Once we got completely away from the club, Max tried getting his brother's club to follow us to cause problems. I don't know what had changed in him, in our friendship, but he was too deep in to their ways of life and enjoyed living like that. Smiles and I got involved in this club, the Oath Keepers. Eventually, Max spouted some shit about how he'd changed and we let him in. He used to be our friend after all, and I tried desperately to forgive him."

Prez stops talking, drinking some more water, and I put my cigarette out. Cain is going to be all over my ass about me smokin' again.

Smiles leans in, "Tell 'em the rest," he grumbles, gesturing to us waiting patiently.

Prez clears his throat, shifting uncomfortably in his chair. "I threatened Max again and told him he better stay away from my Ol' lady this time. Shit was rocky as fuck, Mona found out she was pregnant and I always wondered if it was even my baby. One day I caught him kissing her, and I couldn't handle it anymore. She was pregnant, swearin' it was my fuckin' kid she was carryin', which y'all can tell lookin' at Brently, that boy is definitely mine. Hell, both my kids look just like me an' Mona. Anyhow, I had enough of Max's shit and put him the fuck down. Smiles never forgave me for killin' him, and then Max's piece of shit brother told me that Max should have been President in the Oath Keepers instead of me, along with a bunch of other bullshit. In the end, he threatened that if I ever got another VP, that they would kill my VP. He said that this club could never have another VP until I died and my debt would then be forgotten. It's been so long though, I didn't think that they were keeping tabs any longer and we all know that Ares deserves that spot. Smiles won't take it. After me killin' Max, Mona couldn't move past it. We had Princess and then she left me. I didn't fight her, 'cause it was all my fuckin' fault in the first place, and I couldn't exactly blame her for wantin' to get our kids away. Her sister, Veronica, Smiles' Ol' Lady, took off with her. " He rubs his hands over his stressed out face, eventually coming back to focus on all of us. "Now you wanna tell me what all this shit's about-about what's been goin' on?"

Nodding, I peer at him with newfound respect for overcoming the shit he went through and making his life better. It sounds like he's completely different now, than what he used to be. "Yo, that brother of Max's you mentioned?" I ask, and he looks at me curiously. "He uh, he came to fuckin' collect."

Prez pales at my words, his eyes growing wide in disbelief, "You have to be fuckin' kidding. That shit was like twenty fuckin' years ago! I didn't think any of them even knew where our new clubhouse was. Fuck!"

Smiles grunts. "Ain't no good. That's gonna stir up some shit real quick. You better fix it, ain't gonna stay around this time while you drag us through your shit. I already lost Veronica cause you and Mona couldn't work through it all, ain't gonna lose nothin' else." Prez nods at Smiles.

"Ares, how do you know he came? Did he contact you?"

"That's who cornered the girls, then left the note on the gate and then got to Avery this morning breaking in. Didn't you get my texts?"

"Yeah, I saw them, but Mona's having a real bad time today. She's been sick with a bad fever," he shares worriedly, appearing tired.

Smiles perks up, "Wait! What about Mona? What's wrong with her?"

Instead of answering Smiles, he shares with the whole table. "Brothers, I know I've been absent a lot recently and I'm sorry 'bout it. I haven't been around because my old Ol' Lady, Mona, got diagnosed with cancer. It's pretty fuckin' bad accordin' to the docs. My son hasn't been informed. Mona's afraid after all the shit Brently has had to deal with in the past that he won't take it well. Keep it quiet. I fucked up with her enough in the past; I'm not about to now, when she needs me the most. I hate to leave this shit storm on your shoulders, Ares. I know this is my fault, but you will have to do what you see fit as of now."

"We'll figure it out. You worry about takin' care of Mona and gettin' her well," I mumble, hoping to ease some of the stress he's been carrying.

"What about Princess?" Smiles asks curiously, while Twist taps a near silent beat on the table with his fingers. The brother is always antsy with shit floating in his head.

"Same, still wants fuck all to do wit' me. I wish she would just come chill here some and see I'm not the fucking barbarian she has me painted out to be." He shakes his head, peering down at the table. The man looks so worn out, like he may just fall the fuck out.

Cain speaks for the second time. "Prez, you need to go get a few hours' sleep and some food. Your *own* body won't hold up if you ain't takin' care of yourself." Prez chuckles at Cain's random health advice.

"You've always been the one on us about making the right decisions." He grins, "Christ Cain, you'd think you were the momma instead of London."

Chuckles ring out through the room as everyone relaxes for the first time since we discovered the VP news.

Cain grunts, rolling his eyes, "Well fuck, somebody's gotta take care of you fucking pansy asses or you'd all be feelin' like shit all the time."

"Naw, brother, I think you had one too many lemons with the whiskey you drink," Twist ribs, and we chuckle again.

"All right, all right. Everyone straight now?" Prez inquires, and we nod. "Ares is in charge in my absence. He is, after all, your VP. Treat him with the respect he deserves; he won't lead you astray."

A chorus of 'aye's ring out and church comes to an end.

AVERY

the next day

I'M STILL CONFUSED ABOUT WHAT'S GOING ON BETWEEN THE three of us. I know I love Ares and Silas dearly, but I can't help the worrying thoughts creeping in about if we can have a real relationship. Everything is couples based, but we seem to fit better as three, not two.

I didn't realize 2 Piece' feelings ran so deeply for Ares. I had no freaking idea they were even being intimate; I had the suspicion from before but nothing definite. I would have been irate in any other case, but I love them both, and to find out that they both love me, makes everything seem okay.

Ares can give 2 Piece something that I can't, just like Ares can give me the kinkier side that I crave, whereas 2 Piece can't. At the same time, 2 Piece can give me the stronger emotional connection that I need sometimes, but Ares is more distant. We all fit in this circle that completes the others. That has to count for something, right?

That's another concern I have. Ares has been through so much in his life. I've heard the stories, the whispered things said about him. Will he even be able to have a real relationship with us? We have to talk about it all and set boundaries and what not about everything.

I climb into Cain's car 'Loretta,' closing the door and fastening my seatbelt, as London revs the engine. The car thunders around me, as the 702 horsepower Hellcat begs to be put to use. London stole the damn car again, but this time it's because she wants to ride out to Prez's ex's house and see if we can help out. I don't know the lady, but the guys informed us she's really sick with cancer. Surely she could use someone, even just to tidy her house up or something.

London cranks the radio up, blaring 'Jekyll and Hyde' by Five Finger Death Punch. She and Cain both are hooked on that band. The clubhouse door swings out, opening as Cain and a few brothers storm out. London lowers the window, giving a little finger wave and romping on the gas.

My ass sinks back into the leather seat as the speedometer climbs higher. I've gotten used to London driving like a damn crazed maniac. Usually we're in her little slow ass Civic though, this is a whole new ball park and she seems to be eating it up.

"Shit!" She suddenly shouts, drawing my attention after we've been driving for a few minutes.

"What's wrong?"

London huffs, "They're behind us."

"Wait, who's behind us?"

She squints, staring into the side mirror for a few beats. "Well shit. I thought it was the guys from the club but I don't know who's on the bikes behind us. I don't recognize any of the bikes, and I can't make out their faces—they're covered in bandannas." She rolls her window back up quickly, encasing us in darkness from the tint.

Turning in my seat, I attempt to see if I can make them out any better, but the windows are nearly black and I can't see them. "Should I roll down my window even more to see if I can get a better look out of my mirror?"

"No, I don't think they saw me. For all they know, we're Cain. I don't want anyone to know it's us, just in case. Roll up your window." She orders loudly, turning down the music.

London hits a button on the car in the center of the dash and ringing sounds over the speakers.

"Yeah?" Cain answers loudly. We can hear the rumble of the bike, he must be using his headset.

"Some bikes are behind us. You wouldn't happen to be behind me, would you?" London asks sweetly.

"Nope, but bet your fuckin' ass I'm behind those motherfuckers. Floor it, baby, and lose these fucks, so I can take care of it. Be careful."

"Okay, babe, love you."

"Love you."

The car goes silent as the call clicks off, then returns to the low beat of music. London turns my way, takes a deep breath, and exhaling with a sigh, "Ready, bitch?"

"Let's do it." I nod, grabbing the 'oh shit' handle. She gives the powerful black beast some gas and the car feels like it freaking flies. I wouldn't be the least bit surprised if the tires actually came off the pavement.

London grips the wheel at ten and two, leaning forward, focusing on the road just like the last time she was driving erratically. We speed down the old highway, the exhaust rumbles loudly, almost as if we're in a race. If only that really were the cause; I'm getting tired of these damn chases. First some guy chased 2 Piece and me on the motorcycle which resulted in me getting shot, then London and I race away from the grocery store like our asses were on fire, and now this. I hope London doesn't lose her lunch this time.

"The turnoff is coming up here soon, so take that farm road out to Mona's house."

"We've been driving for thirty minutes already?" I gape at her.

"Hell no, we've been driving way faster than the speed limit, so it's not going to take thirty minutes. I think the bikes are far enough back now they won't see us turning off, but just to be safe I'm going to turn quickly and haul ass again, so be prepared. I hope we don't spin or anything crazy."

"Why on earth would we spin?" I inquire nervously.

"Because that road is dirt just like the back road to the club."

"Shit-fuck, okay I'll say a prayer for us, while you keep watching that road."

Right as I get the words out, she slams on the brakes causing the car to skid and fishtail as she takes a corner at God-knows-what speed.

"Ohhhh shiiittttt!" I groan, and my tummy starts flipping inside. The car makes the turn but the back tires spin over the gravel, swinging the rear end from left to right, before finally getting a good grip and propelling us forward.

"You better not puke!" she calls loudly, and I groan again.

"Don't even say that word, London," I mumble, holding my stomach. I start to take a few deep breaths, attempting to calm down my nerves.

After about ten minutes of straight bumpy, dirt road, we take a turn around a bend full of trees and bushes. An older, light blue ranch-style house comes into view. It has an unattached garage next to it and a chain link fence surrounding the entire piece of land it rests on. Out front an old grey 1979 Chevy pickup sits, appearing forgotten, next to a newer dark blue, Chevy Malibu sedan and Prez' bike. I'm going to guess someone is a Chevy person here and my bet's on Prez.

"Oh thank God!" I huff out, excited to be able to get out of Cain's muscle car. I like the Challengers, but geez, his should be in a class alone.

"Hush your mouth, hooker; I did just fine getting us here safely."

"Um, yeah, you got us here, and it's a freaking miracle Cain's dash isn't wearing my stomach contents right now!"

She laughs, putting the car in park. Prez is on the small front porch with a shot gun before London even gets the car turned off. He's in wrinkly clothes appearing as if he slept in them and then wore them an extra two days. His long blond hair hangs to his shoulders, a greasy mess.

"Fuck, the old man looks tired. Don't say anything about the bikes following us just now, okay?" London observes quietly.

"Sounds like a plan, and quit giving him shit about his age. He's not close to being old, he's just stressed out."

I open the door, clambering out after being sucked into my seat for so long.

"Well heya' Shug', what are you girls doin' out here?" He looks at me, surprised but pleased and props the shot gun against the house.

"Hi Prez, London and I wanted to come check on you, and see if we could maybe help out around here some?"

"Aww, honey, that's sweet of you girls, but I doubt Mona would want any company right now; she's not feelin' too well." He gazes at the ground sadly.

London walks up to him giving him a giant hug, holding him tight and responding quietly, "We know, Prez; that's why we're here. We want to make sure the house is picked up, y'all have some clean clothes, and there's food already prepped to eat. My best friend's granny fought with cancer. Emily's granddaddy always told us about how hard it was during that time. Avery and I want to make sure you have all the tools you need to help Mona get through it and get back to feeling well."

Prez has always been the strong, more silent type, so to see a tear run down that man's face completely shatters my heart for him. He rests his forehead on London's shoulder, bringing her close for a moment, collecting himself.

"My brothers are some lucky fuckers landing the two of you. Come on in and let me introduce you."

London smiles as I approach them. We walk through the front door and Prez throws his arm over my shoulder. Leaning in, he quietly mumbles, "Hey Shug'. Thanks for doin' this. My boys bein' good to ya?"

"No problem, really. Yes, they are being very good to me." I shoot him a small smile and his lips turn up in a miniscule grin. He leans in, kissing my forehead and releases me as he shows us the way to his Ol' Lady.

2 PIECE

My mind was fuckin' racing when Cain came rushin' in, warning us that the girls had taken off again. I had never run to get on my bike so fast in my damn life. I wasn't about to let her go get hurt this time. Next thing I knew, I was surrounded by bikes, as Cain, Ares, and Twist all sped after them alongside me.

Blasting down the highway, I can see the other bikes up ahead of us. Ares gives me the signal and as we get closer, I pull one of my weapons from my boot. It's hard as fuck trying to steer my bike and shoot straight at the same time, but I've been getting better at it. Hell, if it's to keep Avery safe, I'll shoot any fucker in sight.

After a few moments I don't see Cain's beast anymore, so the girls must have been able to lose them. They must be doing well over a buck fifty and that shit makes me nervous as hell, knowing something could happen to Avery if they were to wreck at those speeds.

I watch one biker on a red Harley giving hand signals to his buddies as we start to get closer to them. Their cuts are a deep crimson with a large white fist in the center. *Fuck.* That's an Iron Fists' cut. Glancing to Twist, I see it register on his face on what kind of shit we may be in after seeing just who it is we're following and will be shooting at.

One biker turns slightly, flashing his Glock and I immediately get on one of Are's sides. Being VP, I have to protect him. I would regardless; I love him too much to want anything to happen to him. Cain speeds up, riding on the other side of Ares, both of us shields.

Instead of Twist staying close, he speeds ahead of us getting much closer to the Iron Fists. Shaking my head, I breathe in through my skull bandana, attempting to stay calm and focused.

The fucker in the middle, on the red bike, raises his arm, and clutches his hand in a fist. The guy beside him throws something on the ground. I can't tell what it is because they look tiny.

Ares must know what it is as he screams at a deafening tone, 'Twiiiiissstttt!"

Twist can't hear over the pipes or he ignores him, when suddenly his bike swerves, careening off to the side of the road, and I see his body fly through the air completely off his bike.

"Fuck! Twist!" I yell, slowing my bike down as quickly and as safely as possible. Ares and Cain do the same and stop beside me. I put my kickstand down, jumping off my bike to get to Twist.

"The fuck was that?" I yell back to the guys.

Ares catches up and runs beside me to get to Twist, while Cain stands by the bikes with his gun out in case the fucks decide to come back for a drive-by or some shit.

"It was motherfuckin' shrapnel," he huffs as we run.

"Are you fucking serious?"

"Yep, as a goddamn heart attack."

I can't believe what I'm hearing; those dickwads threw fucking shrapnel at us? Bunch of fuckin' bitches is what they are. Fuck throwing it; I wanna shoot the shit straight into their goddamn bodies. We get to Twist only to find him lying sprawled out and unconscious.

Sitting at his side, I shake him a few times. "Twist, you ugly fucker, wake up!"

Ares grabs my shoulder, "Stop, brother, we don't want to move him in case somethin's fucked up."

"Then what do we do with him?" I'm normally the one playing doctor for the club, but I have no fuckin' clue what to do for him. It's not like he needs me to feed him some whiskey and sew up a few stitches somewhere.

"I think this time we'll have to call an ambulance; fuck if he ain't gonna be mad when he finds out." Ares shakes his head, his gaze meeting mine. "Do you have anything on you?"

"Naw, just my Glocks, but their registered and shit. Nothing in my bags either, I just cleaned the unmarked guns out of my bike the other day."

"All right, I'm gonna go make sure Cain doesn't have any blow on him and then call an ambulance. You stay with Twist until they get here, and I'm gonna have Cain call the girls back, to make sure everything's straight with them. I'm going to send out Exterminator to watch Mona's crib. Make sure none of those fucks stop by. I'mma tell the ambulance he lost control and flew off the bike."

I nod, and he takes off jogging back to Cain and our bikes.

Rubbing my forehead, I peer down at Twist and quietly begin to talk, "Look motherfucker, I may not approve of you with my sister and all, but fuck if you aren't doin' some good with Sadie. Who the fuck knows why, but anyhow she will never forgive my ass if I let anything happen to you. You better be okay, 'cause I love my younger sister, and if you happen to stick around with her, then I reckon' I might could deal with that. Don't go tellin' nobody that shit though, 'specially Sadie."

He's unresponsive and I'm by no means a praying man, but I have to sit here and hope that if anyone's listening that they will take care of my brother. I ain't tryin' to go to no fuckin' funerals. That's the last thing Ares needs to have to worry 'bout, with all the shit goin' on.

After a few minutes of the sound of the wind blowing through the trees, the air is littered with the loud shrieks of sirens as the ambulance nears, along with a police cruiser.

The two medics unload from the truck, going to the back of the vehicle to get supplies. Ares approaches them as the cop starts looking around the road and at Twist's fucked up bike. Fuck, that cop's gonna see that shit in the road and ask questions.

The medics start walking toward me with a portable stretcher board. Ares pulls his wallet out, handing the blond cop a large wad of cash when no one's paying attention. Well, no one but me anyhow. The cop nods, shaking Ares' hand.

"Is he responsive?" the younger medic asks, nodding to Twist.

"No, he hasn't moved at all."

"Okay, thanks. Please step back so we can take a look and get him loaded."

"Yeah man, no problem." I backtrack a few paces. "You know what's wrong with him?"

"Not yet, but hopefully soon," the older medic replies as they secure Twist in a neck brace.

All that jostling around, and yet the brother doesn't stir at all. It makes me worry even more for him and my sister. I don't know what the fuck they have goin' on exactly, but I know she don't need this kinda stress being pregnant and all.

They lift him up and start to carry the stretcher to the ambulance, so I follow along. They load him up as we all stand around and watch.

"You going to the hospital, brother?" I ask Ares.

"No. I just called Scratch; he's gonna come get Twist's bike, and I need to help him load it up. Brother is gonna be lit the fuck up when he sees his bike all smashed up and shit. You should head to the hospital so you can keep me updated, especially if Sadie heads over. Don't want no Iron Fists around to fuck with her, too."

"What about Avery?"

"Trust me 2 Piece, I will make sure she's safe."

"What about that cop? He gonna be a problem?"

"No, that was actually Dom's older brother. He just saw a biker lose traction and wreck. Gotta get this shit outta the road though; I gave him my word."

Nodding, I fist-bump him and Cain, climb on my bike, and follow the ambulance to the hospital.

This shit with the Iron Fists MC better get squared away quick. If need be, I'll take Avery and get the fuck outta here if it means keeping her safe this time. I won't have her gettin' shot or terrorized every time she fucking leaves the goddamn compound. We should be able to keep our women safe, not be the reason they get hurt in the first place.

ARES

2 PIECE LEAVES, RIDING BEHIND THE AMBULANCE AND CAIN steps next to me, "He'll be okay, Ares; you did the right thing, bro."

"I just hope Twist doesn't flip out when he comes to and stab a nurse or some shit. Last thing he needs is to go back to jail. I don't think the brother would come out again functioning. Scratch is on his way. We need to direct people around this shit in the road till he gets here and it all gets cleaned up."

"You gonna call the Prez?"

"No, he's got shit goin' on. He told me to deal with everything for now, so I plan to take care of it. I'll fill him in when I find out how Twist is doing."

"He's gonna fuckin' scalp you, man."

"Nah, Prez will be cool; he knows shit like this happens."

"The fuck we gonna do about the Iron Fists?"

"Well, you call London and tell her not to leave Mona's house until one of the boys escorts them home. If the Fists are watchin', I want them to know we are, too. I'm so fuckin' happy you got a crazy bitch and she steals your cage. Had she been in that silver hunk of shit she has, they'd never have gotten away either time."

"All right. Yeah, I'm thinkin' I need to get her a pink one or some shit. I told her an SUV, but if I end up going that route, then that fucker will be jacked up with some beefy tires and shit."

I chuckle and shake my head. Cain is gonna go broke spoiling the shit outta his ol' lady and kid, but whatever makes him happy. "Then we visit ol' Jake in the shed and find out a little more information about his cocksucking uncle that's stirrin' this bullshit up. We may be able to use the kid as leverage if he means sumthin' to the uncle."

"Good thinkin'."

"I am the VP motherfucker. Not all of us think with our muscles."

He chuckles, shaking his head. "Right, the retired Enforcer, not using his muscles to set someone straight. Sure bro."

Grinning, I wave my hands to flag Scratch over. He slows the black van, stopping near us. Spin jumps out of the passenger side, as Scratch gets out, immediately going for the giant shop broom he has in the back.

"The fuck happened here, brothers?" Spin wrinkles his brow, and it makes his Mohawk shift forward slightly.

"Fucking Fists threw some shit at us," I grumble and he scoffs.

Scratch starts sweeping the shrapnel on the road to the shoulder, thankfully no cars are coming through. This road isn't busy much, part of the reason Prez first picked this place out here to build the compound.

"Help me get Twist's bike in the back of the van."

Spin climbs in the vehicle, turning it around so the ass end is damn near butted up to Twist's bike. He climbs out and we all work together to load up the Harley. Thank fuck we're on the larger side of men or that wouldn't have happened so smoothly.

After that's all taken care of, I climb on my bike, and gesture the guys to head back to the club. I need to think, to plan on what to do with these fuckin' yo-yo's. My pipes rumble loudly, vibrating my thighs as I glide down the highway back to the clubhouse.

Besides all this drama shit, I love my life in the MC. I love knowing that I can do basically whatever the fuck I want. Even now, having Avery and 2 Piece, I feel more complete than I ever have in the past. I have so many damn issues I deal with because of the way things were as a kid, but I'm gonna do everything in my power to not let it all creep up on me and fuck up this relationship I'm having with them.

I hadn't seen Dom's older brother, Brax, in a few years. I knew he was a cop, but I try to stay away from the law. Brax didn't want to take any money, so I told him to send it to his mom. I had heard a few years back she wasn't doin' so well. Kidney disease was gettin' so bad, she could barely leave the house. Poor old woman was stuck in a wheel-chair on a crazy strict diet with a list of complications and meds.

I should visit. I know I'm not how they wanted me to turn out, and Dom's dad partially blames me for Dom turnin' towards livin' the free life on his own bike. His dad wanted both of his sons to be cops, but Dom was troubled inside like me. I don't know what on earth could have fucked with him, as he never shared, but he craved the freedom like I did.

Pulling through the gate, Brently signals that everything has been good, so we ride on through and park. Scratch parks the van next to the big shop and we all help unload the mangled metal. It's gonna take a lot of bending and welding to get her pretty again.

"Who's gonna fix his bike?" Cain glances at me curiously.

"I'd imagine he'd wanna do the shit himself, and if anyone else touches her, he's liable to drive a knife in 'em."

Spin chuckles. 'Fuck that shit, I'll stick to tattoos."

"Good idea," I smirk and head to the little shed where our new friends are still tied up. I can hear the crunching behind me, letting me know I have an entourage in tow.

Once I'm face-to-face with Jake, I can't help but feel my blood start to simmer as I think of his club causing Twist to get injured. The thick air, smelling strongly of urine and sweat nearly makes me gag but I choke that shit down.

"Ran into a little issue today. You know anything about your fuckin' club following around our women? Are they just asking to die?"

He blinks, the wrinkles next to his eyes making him appear more worn down than the day before. "Look, they aren't really my club. My cousin," he gestures to the barely alive guy next to him, "and I don't want to be involved with them at all, but my uncle doesn't give us a choice."

"Naw, I don't fuckin' believe that shit," Cain interrupts, spitefully glaring at Jake.

"I swear to God. He's told us that he will kill us, and if you know my uncle, then you know he will find you and keep good on his promises."

"The fuck he want with our women?" I try again.

"He said they would probably mean something to you and it would get your attention. He didn't want me to hurt them, just to talk to them at first. Then when that bitch hit me with the car, he knew you all meant business. My uncle wanted me to take one of them, then he was hoping we could keep one until you met with him and worked out a deal."

"Well, he done got my fuckin' attention; so much so, I'm ready to find his ass now. I have a brother down, injured right now, that means I can take your cousin as payment, right? Especially now that I hear you was planning on keeping one of our women."

"No way, man. That's his son, he'd go crazy." His eyes widen as that piece of information slips out and you can tell he just realized the importance of what he just admitted to me.

"Hmm." I grunt, going to the bench and finding Jake's cheap black throwaway phone. "Least this piece of shit will still take a photo," I mumble as I scroll through the only two contacts listed. "And I'm guessin' one of these numbers labeled one and two are to reach your uncle," I finish, as I snap a photo of Jake's barely alive cousin. "Let's see which one belongs to him." Smirking, I look at his pale face, taking in his expression that looks as if he just swallowed something rotten.

"Please, you don't know what you will be unleashing if you let him see my cousin like that."

"Yeah? Good. Maybe this motherfucker will get a fuckin' clue that I'm beyond done with his ass."

"You will be starting a war with one of the worst clubs in history. You know this, right? They rape women for sport, they beat their wives and children, fuck they even beat their dogs and you want to send him a photo threatening his own son? Are you crazy? Your club will never survive."

"I ain't fuckin' crazy. 'Cause if your uncle is the type of scum I think he is, well then his kid don't mean a whole hell of a lot to him when it comes to business. He needs to see I'm serious and he needs to respect the fact that I will fuckin' find his ass if I have to and chop that piece of shit into tiny pieces if need be."

"He's the first one; my ma's the second. Please don't send it to her,-- her life's already shit."

I nod and watch him for a few beats to see if he lets on about anything else. Jake swallows harshly staying quiet. Well hopefully, he realizes I'm completely serious. I won't live in a place where my club is being threatened to fuckin' extinction and not do anything to try and save it.

Taking one last look at the grainy photo of the beat up piece of shit, I click send. Now we wait and see what happens.

AVERY

five hours later...

We finally make it back to the compound after a long day of cleaning and cooking. Mona was having a really rough morning, and Prez was just happy to finally get in a little nap, and then be able to spend some quality time with her.

The poor man has been running ragged by the looks of it. He definitely appears thinner than I'm used to seeing. We made him take a shower while we did the laundry and whipped up a large batch of homemade chicken noodle soup. London and I made enough to put a few small tubs in the freezer. Something really easy for Mona to eat, and all Prez will have to do is microwave it. We made a few others, too—creamy broccoli and cheese and cheddar bacon potato, my favorite. Mona may not be able to eat much, but at least when she's feeling up to it, there are some yummy, healthy things prepared. We made sure to make a few quarts of plain chicken broth for when she's having really tough days and can't eat much.

I can't imagine what they must be going though. I feel so bad for them, and every time I see Prez look at her, I swear his heart crumbles to witness her breaking that way. It's a shame that it took her getting this sick for him to finally decide to not wait any longer and just let her go off on her own. They hold a very deep love for each other; I could tell in the way Mona talked about him when she was having small bursts of energy.

I take Lily outside for her to go to the bathroom; poor thing has been locked in her kennel for a long time, unless one of the guys let her out while I was gone. By the looks of it though, the room seems exactly the same as I left it.

I come back in, scouring the place for Ares and 2 Piece. After looking all around the clubhouse, I finally find Ares in his room.

"Hey Air." He lifts up, and I kiss the spot between his chin and cheek chastely. Then I set Lily down to explore his room. She loves Ares and pretty much owns his room. For being such a bad ass, Ares has puppy toys scattered everywhere, and Lily has her own set of dog dishes and dog bed.

"Yo, angel, how was your time at Mona's? Prez get to relax some?"

"Yeah, he got to take a nap and get a shower. We cleaned up Mona's house, made some food, and then let them know we'd stop in again at the end of the week. She's such a sweet lady and damn I bet she's a firecracker when she's well."

"Yeah, she is. Mona is a lot like Sadie and also Mona's daughter,

Princess. Those three are full of fire." I nod and smile.

"How was your day? Where's 2 Piece and Twist?"

"My day pretty well fuckin' sucked. Don't tell Sadie anything yet because 2 Piece wanted to make sure Twist was okay before calling her. You remember when Cain called London 'cause we were following the bikers that were following you and London?"

"Yeah, of course, I remember. London nearly caused me to puke again driving all crazy."

"Well, those fuckers threw shit in the road, causing Twist to wreck. Brother had to go to the hospital, and 2 Piece followed to keep me posted on how he's doing."

"Oh my God, that's terrible. And Sadie doesn't know? She's going to freak out! You guys better tell her soon."

"We don't wanna have her too stressed out, being pregnant and all."

"That's understandable, but you both really have no clue just how much Twist means to her, plus if it were you or 2 Piece, I would want to know."

"I get it, but I'm doing what's best for now."

It takes everything in me to bite back my argument. I'm slowly becoming better with accepting what their decisions are when it comes to this stuff. It's one of the hardest parts of being an ol' lady, learning to keep quiet when they're handling stuff that pertains to the club.

For a while all I did was argue with 2 Piece left and right. I always felt like they were bossing me around and being secretive. Now, I know it's just the way club life is. It still takes some strong self-control though to not throw in my two cents on everything and demand they tell me everything. I know that's not realistic, and I want to respect their rules to live this life with them.

Nodding, I step closer to him and he wraps his arms around me. "I'm happy you came in here, angel," Ares mumbles quietly and it brings a bright smile to my face.

"Oh you're happy, huh? Let's see just how happy you are." I skirt my hand down his firm chest, down over the ridges of his solid abs, loving how his stomach is hard and cut like a warrior's would be.

Eventually, I make it to his cock where I caress him up and down a few times over his solid length. His dick grows in anticipation, and he sucks in a quick breath through his teeth. I bend forward, biting his chest through his shirt where his nipple should be underneath.

"I want you so damn bad, Ares. Do you want me?" I murmur quietly, my hot breath warming his skin through his black shirt, advertising the band 'Highly Suspect.'

His hands come around my waist, pulling me into him so that his hardness rests firmly against my stomach." Avery you have no fucking clue how badly I want you. It's been a while since I ate that tasty pussy out, and that's exactly what I'm craving right now."

He easily flicks my button to my jean shorts, yanking them down my legs as I take my shirt off. Standing in just my black bra and small white thong with polka dots, he growls, clenching his jaw and starts to reach for my panties.

"I'm running out, no more snapping." I pull back slightly pointing my finger, chastising him, as I know Ares will snap the strings easily like he usually does. I think it's like a little fetish he has or something. If I'm wearing underwear, he wants them off, but he wants to break them in the process.

"I'll buy you some more or you can just stop wearin' the fuckin' things."

He winds his fingers in the thin band, yanking me into him and easily snaps the material. I quickly reach behind my back and unclasp my bra, just in case he decides to do the same up top. That material is much stronger, and I know it would hurt like hell.

He grins, watching me, eyes dancing with amusement, then crouches down some, kissing my neck and lightly nipping the tender underside flesh of my breasts. Opening his mouth wide he sucks my nipple and the surrounding area into his mouth, drawing deeply enough it causes a slight shock of pain to jolt straight into my core.

"Aghh, Ares!"

He pulls back, dark eyes hazed over with lust as he repeats it on my other breast, drawing deeply, causing me to moan out. He doesn't try to keep me as quiet like 2 Piece does. Ares is almost the opposite, usually egging me on to be as loud as he can make me, while 2 Piece counteracts him, making me be quiet. The push and pull of them together drives me crazy inside whenever we're intimate. It's like they're music notes working in sync. I hadn't realized it until recently. I've always noticed how well they complimented each other, but thought maybe it was just my lack of experience in threesomes. Now I know it's entirely more than that.

He releases my breast as he begins to make his way down, licking and nipping at my tummy, until he reaches my center. Ares lightly bites the top of my pussy, causing me to open my legs a little in response. Once they are opened the slightest bit, he shoves his face between my thighs, his beard scratching against my skin.

He sucks strongly on the delicate bud of my clit, making me nearly double over, grasping onto his shoulders tightly to keep upright, my fingers dig into his solid muscles. The pleasure is intense, so much so that my arms shoot up to his neck, where I wind my fingers into his dark locks, yanking on them.

He doesn't stop though. It just excites him all the more. He wraps each one of my legs over his bulky shoulders keeping his face trained on my center.

Suddenly he stands up, gripping onto my ass cheeks with his huge paw like hands. I shriek out in surprise, bending so I don't hit my head on the ceiling and he walks us to his bed. Once his feet touch the bed, his knees bend and my back hits the soft bed.

"Angel, fuck, I want you," he gasps, breath fluttering over my throbbing core.

I gape at him, having never experienced a man able to do that to me before. He gives me that roguish grin before he dives back in at the juncture between my legs. Ares thrusts his tongue into my opening as far as he can, and it feels amazing. I'm so turned on I know my wetness must be coating his chin. He loves it like that though and has mentioned before he wouldn't want it any other way.

"Jesus, that feels so awesome!"

"Not Jesus, even if you are an angel, babe," he gruffly replies, his voice deliciously vibrating over each tender part below. "Fuckin' sweetest pussy I've ever tasted, just like sweet cream."

I moan loudly, fighting my voice back from calling out as he plunges a finger into me and pushes me even closer to the brink.

"So close, so close!" I croon repeatedly, my eye's rolling back in delightful surrender.

He plunges in a second finger and circles my clit with his tongue. He reaches up with his free hand and gives a hard pull on my nipple, sending a massive zing straight to my hotspot. It collides with other intense feelings of pleasure, and I see black with little white stars dancing throughout my vision and I explode in one hell of a great orgasm. Holy shit!

Huffing as I try to catch my breath, I gasp, "Ho-ly fu-ck!"

Ares chuckles, his voice thick with lust at my sated outburst. He climbs over my drained body like a limber cat.

Right when he's hovering over me, primed and ready to take more of me, we're interrupted by a harsh pounding on his door.

"Yo!" he bellows irritated and whipping his head towards the source.

The door opens, flooding the room with the cinnamon scent that floats through the clubhouse from the scented vent inserts. Cain's dark head pokes in. "Yeah man, you need to come...oh fuck...my bad!" His eyes grow wide when they land on me underneath Ares and he realizes it's really me. Cain quickly turns so his back is to us. "Sorry 'bout that. Ares, you need to come now, bro. That phone is blowin' the fuck up, and I don't know when you'll get another chance to talk to that fuckin' fist."

"Shit. Okay, give me just a sec to get my pants on." He brushes a damp kiss across my lips, just long enough to leave the taste of myself there and jumps up, his long cock bobbing with his movements as he pulls his worn jeans back on.

"Everything okay?" I know I shouldn't ask him. It's none of my business, but I can't stop it from slipping out. Thankfully he doesn't take it as being nosey, or if he does, he brushes it off.

"Yep." He grins at me again as he pulls his shirt over his head and then slips into his cut.

"You'll let me know about Twist? I don't know exactly what's going on, but you'll be safe, right?" I chatter away as he puts his boots on.

"Angel," he whispers. His gaze softens as he takes the few steps back over to me and kisses me sweetly.

"You'll be safe?" I repeat.

Briefly resting his forehead to mine, he nods. His dark eyes peer into mine as if staring deeply in my soul, his long eyelashes dance as he stares deeply into my soul, "You know you and 2 are mine, right Avery?"

Do I know that? I'm pretty confident deep in my heart; I know that we belong with each other.

"We're yours, Ares," I whisper against his mouth, and he nips my bottom lip before pulling away.

"Then yeah, I'll be safe, and tell 2 Piece to update you on Twist."

"Thank you." I get out, right as he slips out of the room and closes the door behind him. He's never been one for sweet talk, and I have to admit I'm really loving this kinder side of him.

ARES

"**Y**O, BROTHER. THE PHONE?" I MUMBLE AS I CATCH UP TO Cain in the bar.

"Yeah, Brently answered. It's the club phone."

"For fuckin' business? What kind of dick is this?"

Walking behind the bar, Brently nods toward the old white cordless phone resting on the shelf next to some glasses.

Inhaling deeply, I expel the breath clearing my thoughts, as I bring the receiver to my ear. "Yo?"

A gruff voice barks back angrily, "A gift from the Iron Fists. Your club is next." The caller hangs up right as an explosion rocks the windows of the clubhouse.

The brothers hit the floor, quickly drawing weapons out of their boots and holsters. A few take them from the backs of their pants.

Cain turns to me gaping, "The fuck was that?"

Spin cocks his gun. "What's the plan, VP?"

I snatch one of the loaded shotguns from beneath the bar and swiftly hop over the bar top. We keep a few shotguns behind the bar, just for a time such as this.

"Cain, you an' me check this shit out real quick; Spin and Scratch go to the back door just in case any fucks try to breach club doors. Exterminator and Nightmare, grab the sniper rifles and post up on the windows, give us some cover. The rest of ya, you don't let a single motherfucker get past this bar room."

I'm met with nods and multiple yeps, you bets, and okays as brothers get into position, ready to defend the club. I follow Cain to the main door. He opens it slightly doing a quick scan.

"See anything?"

"Shit, bro! It was a fuckin' car that blew up."

A car? Turning back to the room, I ask, "Who the fuck was mannin' the gate?"

Brently speaks up, "The newest prospect." Right, I can't even remember that dudes fuckin' name right now. When I'm done here, I'm gonna be gutting that little twat for letting this shit play out.

"I think we're good to bounce. I don't see no one out there, but it doesn't mean they ain't hidin' an' shit."

"Right. You take the right side, concentrate on your three o'clock. I'll take the left and watch the nine o'clock." I call back, "Night, Ex, watch our twelve."

Exterminator grunts, "bet."

Cain and I make our way out of the club doors and down the few steps, carefully approaching the green sedan all blown to shit and still on fire. There are body parts littered around the area, so clearly someone was in the damn vehicle.

The club door crashes open as Brently comes storming out, running down the stairs, screaming, "Seraphina! Oh God, no!"

"Brently, get back inside bro, it's not fuckin' clear!" Cain barks angrily, quickly taking in the yard of the compound, hoping the President's son doesn't get hurt.

"Noooo, baby, no!" His lip shakes as his knees hit the ground next to the upper half of a mangled body.

"Cain, give us some cover." I step to Brently's side.

"Brently, what is it?"

"It'-it's fucking Seraphina!"

"The girl you were seeing a while back? The one mixed up with the Twisted Snakes?"

He nods as a couple of tears stream over his cheek.

"I thought she wasn't around after that?"

"I-I sent her away. I wanted her to be safe. Look at her hands, Ares."

I run my gaze over her scraped arms that have a few bigger chunks missing out of them until I make it to her wrists. They're tied tightly together with some brown rope.

"She was fucking tied up. They hurt her, Ares," he mutters, his voice thick with anguish.

"I'm so sorry, prospect. You need to get inside though, till every-thing's straight and we can actually talk."

"Everything's straight? Look at her," he yells, "nothing is fucking straight!"

"I get it, Brently, I get it, but you need to get inside and let us take care of it."

"You don't get shit! You don't have a fucking clue what you're talking about!"

"Listen you spoiled little fucking boy, I understand that you're hurt. But you ain't got no fuckin' idea 'bout my life, kid. Now as your VP, I'm tellin' you, for fuck's sake, get your ass inside that fucking clubhouse, now."

Angrily he stands, but pauses and brushes his fingertips over her dirty cheek. "Poor, poor sweet Seraphina," he whispers and walks away, shattered, back inside the club.

Fuck! Just what I need—more damn dead bodies to deal with. Running my hands over my own face, I eventually meet Cain's concerned stare.

"What now, Ares? Everything seems quiet out here."

"Call all the fuckin' brothers that are not here and let them know what just happened. Tell the guys inside to do a perimeter check around the compound. I want to make sure that's the only thing we gotta deal with. Call Smiles and tell him we need this to disappear before someone else sees this shit. I've gotta go check on our guests."

"No problem," he answers seriously, already on his phone calling Smiles to get rid of the debris.

Making my way around the back of the clubhouse, I head straight for the beat up shed. My stomach drops as I take in the chain swinging from the handles, the lock lying on the floor.

Bending, I pick up the heavy metal; it's clear the lock was cut. I already know what to expect when I swing open the door.

Only I had no idea to expect the newest prospect to be strung up in the middle of the shed. He hangs naked, with a symbol burned into his flesh, my small torch lying at his feet. I hope the poor fool didn't suffer too much. *Fuck!* I hadn't even thought to call down to the gate yet. We have to get better security, to keep fuckers out. This is goddamn ridiculous.

As I approach him, my phone begins to vibrate "Yo?" I bark without first checking the ID.

"Brently just called, babbling some bullshit gibberish. My son sounds like he has lost his ever lovin' fuckin' mind. What the fuck's goin' down over there, VP?"

Christ, just what I need. Little boy blue tattling to his fuckin' daddy, while I've got serious shit I need to get fuckin' handled. I don't have time to deal with this bullshit.

"There was a fuckin' car bomb in the parking lot. Your boy came out screamin' 'bout it bein' that bitch who ran with the Twisted Snakes. I thought we got rid of her along with the rest of them during that whole club raid we pulled on them a while back?"

"Hell no, Brently was head over heels for that snatch. Fuck, no wonder he was carrying on. What's the plan then?"

"Well, I just got to the shed. Motherfuckers done split. The new prospect is here hanging in front of me with an "I and F" burned into his chest and stomach. We need to retaliate, no more fuckin' around.

This is a direct threat to the club. I'm so sick of seein' people getting hurt because of these fuckin' yo-yos."

"I know that, brother, but you need to call a vote first. I'm gonna head up there as soon as Mona gets out of this chemo treatment, and I'll help ya. I don't like it that my club's in disarray and I'm nowhere near it to help out."

"No Prez, you stay put with Mona; she needs to be safe and have someone help her."

"We can send a prospect out to take care of her, the club needs me."

"You told me to handle this shit, and that's what I'm gonna do. You take care of your ol' lady, she needs you the most right now."

"Fine, but if something else happens, I ain't sittin' around being a pussy."

"You've always taken care of this club Prez, let me do my part."

"All right son, take care and hit me up if you need sumthin'. My vote by proxy is retaliation after you come up with a plan. No irrational thinkin'."

"Got it."

"Later." He finishes and hangs up.

Fuck, I hope he stays with Mona; she needs him way more than we do right now. We can get by with him away, but I'm not so sure she can. I shoot a massive text for everyone to meet in ten minutes for a church vote. I need to get ahold of some more chapters, too. Get them here as backup, 'cause shit just got real.

Unsnapping my ten-inch blade from my holster, I use it to slit the twine rope that's wrapped around the prospect's throat. His body falls to the floor in a heavy heap once he's free. Slinging him over my shoulder fireman's style, I make my way to 2 Piece's truck, to lay him in the bed until someone can run him over to the funeral home. It's gotta be today though. With the Texas heat, that body will stink and go rancid in no time. Hopefully, the fuckin' birds stay away from him; brother would be looking like road kill pretty quick.

Opening the back, I lift the bottom seat up and get a brown tarp.

Least I can do is cover up the body with it.

"'Sup brother?" Cain startles me, nodding to me spreading the tarp.

"Fuckin' prospect is toast."

"Shit."

Nodding, I finish with the tarp, and then head into the club with Cain following closely.

Once I cross the threshold, I'm instantly bombarded with questions from an anxious Avery, "Air, What was that loud boom? The guys won't let me near the windows or any of the doors and no one will tell me a damn peep!" She finishes, taking both of my hands in hers. "You said you would be careful. Is 2 Piece okay?" she whispers worriedly, her eyes welling up with tears.

Fuck! I don't know how to comfort chicks. "Shhh, angel. You need to get back to the room."

"Back to the room? Ares, tell me what's going on! I've told 2 Piece and I'll tell you, just cause we're fucking doesn't give you the right to boss me."

"Just 'cause we're fuckin'?" I bellow angrily. It sounds like what I said to 2 Piece, and for some reason, hearing it come from her mouth drives me wild with fury. We ain't just 'fuckin'. We are way past that, and she knows it. I'll drive it in deep for her if that's what she needs.

The brothers all stare at us curiously. "Nah, angel, we ain't *just fuckin'*. I laid claim to that fuckin' sweet pussy, so don't get that shit twisted. Now if I tell you to get your fine little ass to that room, then you get your ass to that fuckin' room, ya hear? It's my job to protect this motherfuckin' club, and sugar, your ass is a part of this club, and you belong to me."

I watch, waiting for her smart aleck retort. Her throat moves as she swallows. She nods and gruffly replies, "Well if you claimed it, then kiss me like I'm yours."

"Like mine? Yeah baby, you're mine," I murmur, clasping onto her arms tightly. I lift her small body, carrying her until her back hits the wall. Easily, I let her biceps go, only to wrap my large hand around her dainty throat; I squeeze it lightly as I lean in, owning her lips in front of damn near every brother of this charter.

The room stays silent as their minds race with the fact that I'm claiming her in front of everyone and yet she belongs to my brother, 2 Piece. They don't get it that they both are mine.

After playing with her tongue for a brief time, I pull back, "Say it, angel."

"I'm yours, Ares." She whimpers, thoroughly turned on.

"Louder!" I demand, applying pressure to her throat so she knows I'm completely serious.

She swallows, glancing around the room on each side of my shoulders, "I'm yours, Ares. I belong to you and to 2 Piece," she retorts loudly and I smile proudly. 'Bout fuckin' time the brothers know that.

I step back, kiss her chastely on her mouth, then her forehead, and then release her throat. She doesn't hide her eyes, appearing unsure, when I step away. Instead, she meets every brother's gaze around the room who dare question her declaration. When no one says anything to her or looks at her wrong, she glances at me before silently heading back down to her and 2 Piece's room. That's something else we need to discuss, us living separately. I don't fuckin' like it.

2 PIECE

two hours later...

I hang up with Cain. I gave him my proxy vote earlier, and it looks like we'll get the revenge we crave for this bullshit. My mind still can't get over that the Iron Fists killed the young prospect and breached the compound without anyone knowing about it. That's way too close to the people that mean the most to me. We are getting more people to man the entrance, end of story. I will talk out of my ass to make it happen if needed.

The white machines beep as they monitor vitals, echoing around the sterile hospital room as Twist sleeps. Luckily, the brother finally woke up once he was in the ambulance. The medics said they had given him a little oxygen, and after a few minutes he woke, flipping out. They sedated his ass and threatened to throw him in jail or the psych ward if he didn't calm down. I guess Twist thought that was hilarious and cackled half way to the hospital like a fuckin' loon, finally passing back out. I don't know if Twist could handle another stint in jail, and the psych ward won't help at all. Brother would probably end up getting popped for killing a few other crazies in that place.

Cain's words replay in my mind about the explosion in the fuckin' parking lot. I'm sick of this shit. The brothers should have just listened to me when I told them to find the fucks after Avery and London were confronted at the store.

Twist's fingers tap as he pounds out a silent beat on the bed, no one is ever privy to knowing. Brother always has shit running through his mind; I guess in this case even when he's sedated. My thoughts brake as the hospital door opens and an older lady in a white coat enters. She carries a clipboard with papers she scans after she checks each machine.

"He all right?" I break the silence, nodding to Twist.

"Yes, Mister...?

"Silas ma'am, please just call me Silas."

"Okay Silas, your friend here took quite a spill. Do you know what that could have done to his body?"

"Yes ma'am, I was riding alongside him."

"I see. Perhaps you should think of giving up the motor bikes?"

I glance down over my cut and chuckle. Not being disrespectful, but if she had any idea what all these patches adorning my leather meant, she'd know I'm in for life. Twist, too. That brother eats, breathes, and sleeps the MC.

"Naw ma'am, just hoping my brother is all right."

"Right. Well, he bruised some bones and cracked a rib, but as long as he keeps it wrapped up tightly, he will be fine."

"So when's he gonna wake up?"

"I'd say after the horse tranquilizer wears off," she replies, winking before she leaves the room.

I think the old lady was just flirting with me. It probably was a damn horse tranq with that crazy fucker. I dial Avery's number to check how she's doing with all this madness. I bet my poor girl's nerves are frazzled to no end with her nosey self.

"Hey, Silas." Her sweet voice carries over the line.

"Hey, Shorty. How's shit? You good?"

"Yeah, I'm okay. I'm hanging out in our room until they all figure out what's going on."

"That's real good free bird, glad you're staying off their backs."

She huffs, and then whispers, "I miss you. I wish you were here with me through this stuff."

"I know Avery, so do I."

Twist starts to stir, grumbling as he begins to finally wake up again.

"I gotta go; I'll be back to the club as soon as possible."

"I love you, Silas."

"You, too," I reply, hanging up.

"Errrmmmm. Bastards. Fuck you. Bastards."

"Twist? Brother, you good?"

"Hmmm?" His eyes open, meeting mine.

"You straight?"

"Hmmmpf. Yep, fuckin' dicks shoved a goddamn needle into my arm."

Chuckling, I step to his bedside and undo the buckles on the restraints they had holding his wrists in place.

"Seriously? Fuckin' restraints?"

"From what I got, you scared the little medics, and they thought you was gonna hurt somebody when you woke up again."

"Fuckin' right. I told 'em I ain't need no damn hospital. I need to get back to Sadie, I know she's gotta be beat. Bitch is always on her feet."

"My little sister is fine. She's pregnant, not incapable. Don't let her hear you callin' her a bitch neither brother, you won't have any nuts left when she's done with ya."

He grins, nodding, "I know, crazy ass chick."

"You good to ride? Doc said you have a broken rib and once you stop being a pussy you'll be okay."

"I'm no pussy, motherfucker. You're just mad 'cause I'm older and wiser than your pretty boy ass."

"Whatever man, I catch shit from all y'all whether I'm older or younger, don't give a fuck. You're just hatin' 'cause you look like you went through a damn meat grinder."

"Fuck."

"Yup. Now we bouncin' from this joint or what?"

"Yeah, yeah, give me a sec."

I hand him his clothes and he slips the pants on, gritting his teeth as he bends.

"You got anythin'?"

"Naw, man. Cain took the blow that was in your saddle bag."

"Figured." He grunts, slipping his feet into his boots. He takes a deep breath, and then rips the IV straight out of his arm.

"Shit, man!" I call and he shrugs.

Grabbing up the gauze and wrap from the small cart next to him, he winds it tightly over the bloody mess on his wrist from the IV. I know that shit had to hurt, but he just goes on like he didn't really feel it. I hand him his cut as he gets his dirty, torn T-shirt over his head. He slips it on just as the nurse makes it to the room.

"Oh, sir! Please lie down! The doctor needs to come check you over, please!"

"I'm outta this fuckin' rat hole. Only place you're takin' me is to fuckin' jail if you don't clear outta my way," Twist growls, and the poor nurse moves to the side so he can pass.

"Please, sir, let her come go over your injuries."

"Not fuckin' happenin' red, doc already paid me a visit."

The red headed nurse's cheeks tint with his nickname and boom, Twist is out the door. I follow quickly. He doesn't know yet that his bike isn't here, so this may be interesting.

"Come on, brother, we're parked over in 'B.' The prospect brought you a bike."

"What are you talkin' about?"

"Your bike is trash man, I'm sorry."

"Ah, fuck. Probably about time I start lookin' for a new one anyhow."

"Seriously?"

"Yep, gotta get a bitch seat."

"You need to slow the fuck down with Sadie, brother."

He huffs and stays quiet. I'm being hella cool about him and my sister, considering I should be slitting his throat for messing with my baby sister.

I mount my bike and he climbs on next to me, riding Cain's old cruiser. I send him a glare, 'You know I oughta beat your ass. I will if you fuck with her and that kid.'

"I ain't doin' a motherfuckin' thing, brother, but helpin' her out when she needs it."

I nod as I give the throttle a little gas, heading out of the parking lot to the main street. We cruise for a little while, not really rushing since I know Twist has to be sore, even if he won't admit it.

Some dick decides to pull off the side of the road right in front of us, driving around twenty miles per hour. Fucking assholes. It's stupid idiots like this that causes wrecks, pulling out really slow in front of people. What ever happened to being respectful? My temper flairs as I get angry and veer around the vehicle. The dick dawgs me as I pass his window, me peering inside.

"Little fuck," I shout and kick his door.

He rolls his window down and shouts something but I can't hear him over my pipes. Twist comes up beside me and we rev really loud. The douche nozzle rolls his window up, shaking his head. Fucking pussy, next time don't act ballsy if your just gonna roll your window back up. Twist kicks the guy's car and we speed off.

Twist and I arrive at the clubhouse and there must be fifty bikes parked outside. I'm guessing they also voted to pull in some more charters seeing as we're going up against the Iron Fists.

Twist and I back our bikes into line along the club, scanning the area, you can never be too careful. The burnt car Cain spoke about is missing. It's so dark out now, you wouldn't be able to tell there was even a dark spot from the bomb if it weren't for the bright ass lights shining everywhere. Full security lockdown.. Means a bunch of lights all over everything, cameras monitored twenty-four hours a day, the gate locked, and only opened by approval each time.

"The fuck's goin' on, 2 Piece?"

"Car bomb in the fuckin' compound. Cain went ape shit over the phone, real serious stuff here. I'm guessin' the other charters are here to help us with retaliation."

"This shit better not blow back. So fuckin' tired of women getting' hurt cause of fucking twats."

"I feel ya brother, trust me." I grumble and bang on the club door.

In full lockdown the club doors are locked and only answered after a check in from the gate and even then, the door is still opened with a shotgun pointed in your face.

The heavy door creaks open, with Spin holding a gun through the opening. Once he sees us and looks behind us, he opens the door enough so we can come inside. The bar is packed full of members. Most are from the surrounding charters, but a few really harsh, mean-looking fuckers' cuts advertise Nomads. Ares called in a few of the big dogs. He must be on a mission, and boy do I feel for the person in his path.

The cuts all advertise fellow Oath Keepers MC members. There are brothers here from Louisiana, Colorado, Arizona and Texas. I'm guessing they all came straight from a rally happening in Austin. We were gonna go, being it's so damn close but all this shit started poppin' off. These Iron Fists obviously didn't realize we'd have backup an hour down the road and not spread further out like usual.

If needed, we can always call our brothers in the Forsaken Liberty MC, too. They are located over near Lufkin, Texas and will help us out anytime we need it, too. Let's hope it doesn't come to us calling charters in from all over the U.S. or asking our brothers from other MC clubs to come help out.

"Spin," I greet him, walking past the shotgun.

"2." He chin lifts then turns to Twist. "You good, brother?"

"Fuckin' peaches an' cream, Spiny."

Spin rolls his eyes, locks the thick metal door, and heads back to his table. He has the little Asian he favors, resting in the seat next to him.

I'm met with a shrill voice that I can only describe as my sister's 'you're gonna die, yell.'

"Twist! My God! What on earth happened to your face?" Sadie gapes, running up to him, like a worried mother.

I should have had someone warn Sadie that Twist has a road burn patch on his arm and his nose is busted to shit. He hasn't given it any time to heal up yet, splitting from the hospital like he did, so it looks like he has two noses with it being so swollen.

"Ice! God, we need some ice!" Sadie shouts again, and takes off quickly toward the kitchen, her pregnant belly making her waddle as she goes.

London comes up to us, concern written all over her face, "Twizzler! You okay, love?"

"Ah, cupcake, you know I'm good."

London nods, giving him a small kiss on the cheek. "If you need anything, just ask."

"Thanks darlin', I will."

She smiles briefly, and then makes her way back over to Gain's lap. Twist turns to me, "Thanks for sittin' with me."

"It's nothin', brother."

Sadie enters the room, scanning the crowd like a mad woman, and I duck out before she can rip me a new one. There are only two people I really want to see after all of the shit that went down.

ARES

2 PIECE IS LYING ON THE BED WHEN AVERY AND I STEP INTO their room. I had gone out back with her to walk Lily. She definitely doesn't need to be by herself, especially after those two fucks escaped. They must have been dragged out because the one guy was damn near dead. At this point, I don't want any of the women being left alone outside of the club.

Lily runs over to 2 Piece when she notices him, so excited, her little stub of a tail wags rapidly. He chuckles and she finally calms down after a moment, seeking her dog bed full of fluffy, squeaky toys.

"Ain't nobody gonna believe you're a badass with a room full of squeaky toys, brother." I razz him and he flips me off in return.

Avery sits beside him, grasping his hand, happy to see him. "Silas, are you okay? I was freaking out with the wreck and everything."

"I'm straight, Shorty. You good after all the shit that went down here?"

"Thankfully, Ares was here, so I was okay. I missed you, though."

"Aww, I missed you, too, beautiful."

Clearing my throat, I sit on the bed, opposite side of 2 Piece. "We ah, we need to talk over some shit, yeah?"

He peers at me seriously for a second, and then nods briefly, knowing we all need to discuss our situation more.

"I don't like us staying apart," I begin. "I like it that we have our own space if needed, but I don't want to sleep without you two anymore. I wouldn't ever stay the night before 'cause I was tryin' to keep myself distant and shit, but obviously that ain't gonna happen anymore, you feel me?"

"Yeah and I feel the same," 2 responds gruffly.

"I agree. I want you both close," Avery answers and bites her bottom lip.

"What you thinkin'?" 2 Piece turns back to me.

"We could get a house together? Maybe four bedrooms, so we each got our own space then one room for all of us?"

Avery smiles brightly, "So, you've thought about this a lot?"

"I did today when all the shit went down and we were waiting for Twist and 2Piece to get back. I'm tired of hiding. I want the club to know we're together. I don't know how they will handle it an' all, but I'm done pussy footin' around."

"I'm cool with getting' a place. Shorty?"

"Yes, I am, too. I think it's a great idea! And, well, I'm pretty sure the club knows how you feel about me after earlier."

"What happened earlier?" 2 Piece peers curiously at me.

"I may have kissed her and made her loudly declare that she's mine. Boy, the fuckin' dirty looks the brothers were sendin' me were crazy."

He chuckles, "Good, I'm glad. Probably gave them all a lot to talk about today with that one. I think we should have everyone together and let them know at once, that we aren't a couple, but a three."

I nod, my stomach racing with the excitement of everyone finally knowing that the three of us are together—really together. No more club pussy for me, and now my angel will have two Ol' Men. She'll receive even more respect that she deserves from the brothers.

"When are we going to move?" Avery questions, enthusiastically. I'm a little surprised, since she's grown to love the club and being around the brothers. I think she enjoys them all because they know what it feels like to want to be free and not judged about every little thing.

"How 'bout we look for a spot after this shit is taken care of?"

"Sounds good, brother."

"Okay," Avery smiles, and I can't help but relish in the memories from earlier—the ones where my tongue was deep inside her center.

Gripping onto 2 Piece's bicep, I pull him to me. His eyebrows shoot up in surprise. After being away from each other all day, our lips finally meet, and I feel complete as my tongue caresses over his.

He makes me feel whole, and Avery makes me feel like I'm finally at home.

An electric guitar rings through the air, coming from the thin wall behind the bed. My guess is that Twist decided not to party. Some nights when he's too busy thinkin' 'bout shit, he'll lock himself in his room and ring through some crazy guitar pieces. The brother could seriously be someone famous if he wanted, but he won't ever play for anyone..

We've all walked by his room, hearing the insane sounds he can produce and have each asked him to play. The answers always the same, "nope." No one knows what the fuck happened to him, but whatever it was, it sure did break the man.

2 Piece pulls away, licking his lips as his eyes blaze with an inferno. "Sounds like Twist is playing his songs. Poor guy, somethin' must have stirred some shit up with him today."

"Ain't my business," I shrug, wanting to concentrate on him and not Twist's shit.

Avery runs her fingers over my bicep, pulling my attention to her. "Don't you ever wonder what happened to him?"

"Nah, angel, not really my thing to pry into shit. If any brother wants to talk and shoot the shit, then I'm game, but ain't gonna speculate."

"He has night terrors some nights," she says softly. "He screams these gut wrenching sounds. Sometimes it's names, but I can't completely make them out. He never answers if I try to knock on his door, either."

2 Piece grumbles, "Shorty, I told you that ain't our damn business. That's just another reason he don't need to get too close to my sister; she don't need to deal with more shit."

Shrugging, finally giving up the Twist subject, Avery pulls her light blue sundress off, exposing herself completely to us. She literally steals my breath away with all of her lightly tanned skin on display, and all I can do is groan in sweet surrender.

"That whole time I was walkin' the dog with ya' you didn't have nothin' on under that fuckin' little dress? For fuck's sake, angel, I would have fucked you against the goddamn wall already."

"Well, y'all keep telling me to stop wearing the stuff underneath, so I thought I'd try it out." She grins mischievously. 2 Piece and I are already starting to shuck our clothes, throwing them in all different directions.

"You boys seem a little eager; I'm guessing I made the right decision then?"

2 Piece growls and I chuckle, "Angel, we ain't no boys. I keep tellin' ya we're men sweetheart. Let us show you how good we can make you feel."

She knee walks towards me on the bed. She's so damn sexy, and she has no idea just what she can do to a man. She comes close enough until her face is level with my waist. She cups my balls in her hand, grazing her nails over them lightly, making them tighten up in delight.

"Come here, 2," I grumble and gesture him towards Avery and me.

He circles around the foot of the bed until he stands beside me in all of his gorgeous, tattooed naked glory.

"Fuck, the two of you are so goddamn sexy," I say just as he bites harshly into my shoulder. He fucking loves biting, and it turns me on like crazy.

I yank on his brown hair, forcefully bringing his face right in front of mine. His excited pants whisper over my lips, and I can smell whiskey on his breath. "Stand on the bed; it's my turn to taste you."

He steps up, holding my shoulder for support, and stands on the bed. His cock is much easier for me to reach, closer to my level now. He balances, raising his hands to rest his palms flat against the ceiling for support. His body on full display at that angle is a goddamn work of art. His tattoos stand out in bright contrast to Avery's flawless skin, and his lean muscles accent each curve in his stance.

Avery rests on her knees, pretty auburn head bobbing up and down as she goes to town sucking my dick. I move one hand in Avery's hair, reminding her that I'm paying attention to her as well. My other hand I reach around, gripping onto 2 Piece's firm ass cheek and bend to take his cock into my mouth.

I hollow out my cheeks as much as I can, relaxing my jaw and throat. His dick slides easily in and out of my mouth, the tip hitting the back of my throat.

"Oh fuck, Ares," he croons, watching me. Avery groans hearing him moan in pleasure.

I damn near grit my teeth as her mouth vibrates around my shaft, pulling back and licking all over the sensitive head. My teeth graze over 2 Piece's cock as I nearly forget to keep my mouth open through my own pleasure.

After a few minutes, I pull back, letting his cock slip out of my mouth. 2 Piece's muscles are strained, nice and tight from holding onto the roof and riding through the pleasure. His abdominal muscles clench and release with each deep breath he expels, and it makes me want to nip each ridge.

"Avery," I clear my throat as my cock hits the back of her mouth and it takes my breath away shortly at the insanely good sensations. "Get on all fours," I demand and she quickly complies. She releases my dick and my ass muscles instantly relax. I had them flexed so tight from the pleasure, it's amazing I didn't get a fuckin' cramp.

"Time to suck 2 Piece's cock, beautiful." She moves as I order her, getting into place in front of him, providing me with the perfect position to take her from behind. I line myself up, ready to take her sweet spot. Gripping her small hips, I plunge my long cock into her tight center.

Bitch feels like she was designed perfectly to fit my big veiny dick. When you find a pussy like that, it creates a frenzy inside of a man. The insatiable need, to have yourself inside of her all the time, filling her up with your seed and claiming her for yourself. That shit will drive a brother fuckin' crazy, thinking about it all the time. I see why 2 Piece gave in and kept her, she's fuckin' unforgettable. Not only when I'm inside of her, but when she's busy giving me some sass and flirting with me, too. Avery's exactly the kind of woman I want to see myself with in the future. Between her and 2 Piece, I find the perfect balance of what my body needs.

"Ohh!" She moans around 2 Piece's dick as I bottom out in her little hole, 2 Piece's eyes bulge slightly. I know that shit feels beyond amazing when she attempts to speak with your cock still in her mouth, or when she swallows and her throat grazes the tip of your dick. Fuck, that thought alone makes me get wet with pre-cum.

"Fuckin' blissful, man," I gasp in between thrusts.

He nods shortly, agreeing with my statement, attempting to keep his mouth closed as his cheeks redden with the incredible feelings. Avery's skilled little tongue will bring a man to completion, in just a few minutes. You have to really work on enjoying the pleasure, but also chant in your head to not cum too damn early. I think the little minx does that shit on purpose. Braggin' rights or some crazy shit chicks do.

2 Piece clears his throat, pulling Avery's head up. "Okay shorty, lean back into Ares, it's my turn."

She rests against me so her back is flush to my chest. Wrapping my arm around her waist and then my other over her tits, I hold her to me still steadily rocking into her. She lays her head back onto my shoulder, watching 2 Piece in front of her.

She's in the perfect spot, exposing the lightly tanned soft skin of her neck. Her body is riddled with little nibble marks from 2 Piece always biting her, but I think it's sexy as fuck to know she's marked. She belongs to us, and I want everyone to know it. Licking up her sweet skin on her throat, I clamp down, nibbling lightly with my teeth, but sucking strongly, creating a rich, dark red mark, marring her where everyone can easily see it. I hope she doesn't get upset over it, but I'm sure she'll realize I did it on purpose.

2 Piece sits in front of her, bending to put his face in her perfect juncture. I watch his tongue as it licks up and down, quickly licking her bud like a kitten after some cream. It's so fucking hot watching the man you love licking the woman you love's pussy. There's nothing like it, especially when you're being included in it all.

"Ohhhhh!" She cries out and I twist her chin to me, taking her mouth in a strong kiss, muffling her cries of pleasure, just how 2 Piece likes it.

I continue to pump into her, the ridge of my cock head, drawing her back toward me as I pull it out, just to sink it back into her. Occasionally, she attempts to cry out, but I swallow each plead of pleasure, taking all that I can get, owning her as 2 Piece eats her pussy.

She can't take much more of the constant attention to her body, and I feel her little hole start to squeeze me tightly, telling me that she's ready. Her body speaks to mine, ordering me on what to give to her, on what all I can take. Only I vow to take everything. I want it all, her body, her heart and her fucking soul. Mine, all mine.

Releasing her lips, I clamp my eyes closed tightly, bending my head as I pant savagely, making myself attempt to hold back. These emotions bubbling up belong to the fuckin' monster buried down deep, and I know if I don't stay in control right now, I will seriously hurt her. Crushing Avery's delicate little body as I claim her like some fucking rabid beast is not something I want her to experience.

"I love you, Ares," she croons lovingly against my ear. Her silky voice washes over me, and it's like a warm bath, surrounding me in what I need. She instantly calms me, her voice centering me, bringing me back to just focusing on her.

"Love you, too, Angel," I grumble as I give in to my cock's blistering need to spill itself inside of her. It's almost as if I have this need inside to spread my seed into her a much as possible. I've never thought of children before—being way too fucked up inside—but suddenly I can't help the flashes of images fluttering through my mind, imaging her belly swollen with my babe growing inside of her.

My come spurts with that last thought, coating her insides in everything that I have. I'll give her anything I possibly can. Every-thing...just so she's a part of me.

"Fuck," I murmur, pulling back after a moment, as I can't get those thoughts away from my mind. I don't know what's fuckin' came over me and it's trippy. I didn't even want an ol' lady, and now I'm imagining knocking one up.

I step back from them, letting them have their own time. I'm finished, but they're still lost in the haze of their own orgasms.

I sit, propped against the headboard and watch as 2 Piece lays her back, sliding into her easily as she's still full of my come. He sucks on her small tits, making sweet love to them with his mouth. They are utterly beautiful together.

I can't believe my come doesn't bother him being in her like that, but his face is turned to bliss as he experiences the amazing feelings I was just going through while deep in her cunt. It wouldn't bother me either, honestly. Having his warm cum on me, the man I love, while deep inside the woman I love, sounds like perfection.

I'm so fuckin' lucky they feel the same way about me. This wasn't a relationship I ever believed possible, but fuck if I wouldn't give them every single piece of me if I needed to. I just fuckin' love them. I have to squash this bullshit with the Iron Fists. I can't handle the fact that these two could be in serious danger. I will kill the entire goddamn club of the fuckin' Iron Fists if needed. I'm done with them fucking with the people who matter the most to me. Time for a plan.

Church

two weeks later...

Slamming the gavel down and looking to the faces of my brothers surrounding the table, I go over the plan we mapped out one last time. The room is damn near full with everyone, either back in town or still here from the club lockdown we implemented two weeks ago.

The club stayed locked down tight for three days, not letting anyone come or go. Everyone got bored and pissy, but it was worth it for their safety. We needed everyone here in the compound in case shit went down.

Prez and Nightmare stayed out at Mona's house to make sure she was safe, and I damn sure wasn't 'bout to let the Prez be without some sort of fuckin' protection. He wasn't keen on it, but eventually relented when the members backed me up on the decision. Mona is way too sick to be movin' around, so it was the next best thing we could do to keep them safe.

When nothing else happened to the club or any of its members and everything was quiet, we let up, but most of the brothers still stayed with their families a lot, to make sure they were safe. The loners took off to do whatever it is they do, needing a dose of freedom and have since returned now that we know a little more about the Iron Fists and what we have to do.

We've discovered that they originate out of Cali. They have a smaller Texas chapter to the west, between Odessa and El Paso, which we already knew about. The Texas chapter has about twenty members, a bunch of really nasty fuckers. The brothers were even more on edge hearing that the MC is a cesspool of rapists and women beaters.

I'm sure they have loved having free rein being located out in bum fuck Egypt. There is nothin' out there, but dirt and boring ass highway. I'm fairly surprised we haven't run into them on any of our runs down I-10. That being said, they're a long way from home, being here in our area.

I so badly want to torch their fuckin' club, but no matter how much we dig around, we can't seem to find a location for anything. It's like they just come up out of the fuckin' ground and then disappear again. We're going to have to pay them a little visit at the motel they're staying in before they do something else or fuck off to God knows where.

The motel wasn't hard to find. A few phone calls around Austin to other surrounding clubs confirmed that they had seen an Iron Fist on occasion. The other clubs were happy to give up the areas they had spotted them in, being that the Oath Keepers are old friends with many clubs and they're not fans of the Iron Fists either. Once we had a few spots to search, we found their bikes in no time. We even confirmed it with a scared, brown haired hotel clerk of the Sunshine Inn a few days ago, who looked like he was gonna piss his pants when five of us piled into the hotel lobby. Since then he's called every day to check in and keep us updated on whether any more or less of those fuckers are around there.

A plan started to formulate, while we were taking in the shithole conditions and the location being more on the outskirts of town. I've had some time to think of different approaches, and I think we finally have shit figured out. It's been long enough that they more than likely think that we aren't gonna retaliate or that we haven't a fuckin' clue where the ass clowns are located.

Yesterday we took their bikes and dropped them off at Rudy's old chop shop garage in a ghetto part of Austin. Rudy can have the bikes scrapped in no time, that'll give us a little extra cash to give to the family members who had to miss work due to the useless fuckin' around. It'll also make those pricks immobile besides maybe jacking a cage to use.

"Brothers, everything went down without a hitch last night, taking the bikes. So far there's been no blowback. I'm assumin' either the dumb fucks haven't stolen any cages yet, or they're plottin' something.

We need to strike soon, before they have a chance to get too creative." I'm met with multiple grunts. Cain eats his lemon wedges with no reply, and Twist anxiously taps away on the large table in front of him.

Smiles leans forward, resting his elbows on the hard surface, "I think it's best if the Nomads handle this."

2 Piece sputters and the Nomads sit up straighter, their interest peaked. "No fuckin' way. They attacked mine and Cain's Ol' Ladies; we get to collect on that debt, brother."

"2 Piece." Nightmare growls, "Smiles is right. If this blows back on the town some way, it's better if we're responsible for it versus the club that resides here."

2 Piece turns to me, eyes pleading for me to side with him, but I can't. As much as I would love to get my revenge on these scummy fuckers, I have to do what the Prez would do.

"Look, I have to think of what's best for not only the club, but also the towns around us. If anything comes back afterward, then the Iron Fists will go after the NOMADS, taking the Fists away from the main compound and keeping the city safe along with our families." Smiles nods his approval, while 2 Piece silently stews.

Twist cracks his knuckles, causing everyone's eyes to glance towards him, "I want in."

Cain scoffs, "You're no Nomad, brother."

"Maybe I oughta' be? Sick an' tired of fuckin' pussies."

2 Piece's fist slams onto the table, with a boom, causing it to shake. "Shut the fuck up, Twist, for fuck's sake. You ready to dip out so soon, after getting' all cozy an' shit with my baby sister, motherfucker?"

"Mind your own business, 2." Twist smirks, egging him on. They've had this back-and-forth bullshit goin' on now for far too long. Eventually it'll come to blows or 2 Piece will shot him, if they don't start burying it.

"All right, let's get back to the issue at hand. Twist, we gotta vote if you're serious about goin' Nomad, and then you gotta call in for a transfer. Take a few days to drink and sleep on it." Twist nods, satisfied for the time being.

"Ex, Night, you boys are familiar with the pig farm. You remember how we took the Twisted Snakes MC out there?" They both nod. "Same deal, take them there alive if possible, chop them up, and feed them to the pigs. We don't need any of them out floating around. See if you can get any kind of information out of them first."

Exterminator checks me over, scanning my face carefully with his menacing gaze, almost as if he's looking for something. "Anything specific we supposed to be finding out?"

"No. In fact anything you find out will be a bonus. Just finish these fuckin' Fists; I'm ready to move onto other business."

Smiles peeps in, "Guns."

"Yes brother, we're due for another run. We need to make some bank. Cain, have you spoken to the Russian?"

"Yeah bro, he's ready; he has a new shipment of some specialty guns. It's supposed to be some Call of Duty type shit. I briefed 2 Piece on it already."

"2 Piece, what's the plan?"

"I spoke to Tate, told him to hold on to it all, that we had us a little shit storm goin' on right now, but that someone would be heading to Tennessee soon for pick up."

"Good. I still don't want anyone alone, especially the females. Not even to walk outside or take a piss. They are more vulnerable right now especially with shit 'bout to pop off. Prez's buddy from the fencing company came by. The gates have been updated along with the new razor wire along the tops. Ol' boy put an electric wire running through it, so we can have it on anytime we want. And, if anyone cuts the fence, we'll know that the connection is lost. We added in a few more cameras and Exterminator has been monitoring the feeds. That should put an end to motherfuckers breaching our compound walls. If it happens after this, I'mma build a goddamn moat around this bitch. Anything else?"

Everyone remains quiet, a few smirking at my moat comment. They all know I'm beyond sick and tired of dealing with this fuckin' gate bullshit. I press on about my personal issue. "I need to bring something to the table. I know some of you have pretty well figured it out and all, but then some of you gossip like a bunch of fuckin' school girls, too." Glancing over at 2 Piece again, he grins, ready for me to get it out in the open. "We wanted to make this shit official sooner but with everything happening, we haven't had everyone in one place at the same time since the fuckin' lockdown.

"Avery, 2 Piece, and I are in a relationship. Avery is no longer just the property of 2 Piece. I'm officially laying claim. The bitch belongs to the both of us. I expect you all to show her the respect she deserves being whom she belongs to. She's the VP and SAA ol' lady, for fuck's sake. Besides London, she's the top bitch around here. Y'all got shit you need help with for functions and what not, ask those two. I know they would be thrilled to help out any way they can. Anybody got shit to say 'bout it?"

Cain chuckles, "Yeah, bro. It's about fuckin' time!" He was one of the few who had figured it out already and actually seemed really supportive, thank fuck. Brother's basically my best friend, and I would have hated to lose him 'cause he couldn't get on board with my choice.

"Yeah, yeah, little dick, don't razz on me." At that, the room lightens and a few more chuckles sound off. Brother's grinning happily at 2 Piece at me.

"All right, we good?" I gaze around the table. I'm met with stares full of respect. With the news I just shared, it's surprising. I wasn't even sure they would accept my feelings at all, but in reality they seem to support me more just bein' real with them about it. I should have known, that's one thing about the Oath Keepers, there's no fuckin' judgment about shit like this. I seemed to forget that along the way, trying to make myself believe that I didn't give a shit what anyone else thought, when in the end, I *do* care. This is my family, a room full of brothers, who have devoted their time and lives to protecting me if needed. The pit in my stomach gets a bit smaller with another thing finally coming to rest.

I nod and slam the gavel down, calling church to an end and dismiss them. The men take me off guard as they walk up behind me, each slapping me on the shoulder or fist bumping me as they head to the door. The feeling in my stomach eases even more. Usually Avery is the one who calms the anger inside; but today, it's my brothers.

The group of nine Nomads stay behind as everyone shuffles through the door in search of something to drink and smoke.

"Ares?" Nightmare gazes at me quizzically, as the Nomads stand, coming to surround the table. Their bodies are very large and imposing, they all make me feel like I'm not overly big myself, like we're each supposed to be this size.

I take in their hard faces, some marred with scars, others with wrinkles from a rough life on the road. One thing they all have in common though, is that they're some scary motherfuckers and that's saying some shit coming from me. They aren't the typical Oath Keeper MC fucked up, no these men have lived dangerous lives, a few having been on many deployments overseas, some having gone through years of hard time. I'm pleased to have them around my table, ready to take care of business for the club.

"'Preciate y'all coming to take care of this problem. I fuckin' hate these little pricks and would do it myself, but with the Prez out, I think this is what he'd do."

"Ain't nuthin', man," the tall, light-haired Viking-like Nomad, called Zeus, mumbles.

"Right, so do y'all have a plan on how to catch these sneaky fucks, besides what we've already pulled on them?"

A few chuckle darkly and a red-headed brother called Scot chortles, "Aye, let us handle it, yay? We will fock some lads up, bet your arse, boy."

Standing, I make my large presence known as well. Just because I was sitting, doesn't mean I'm some kind of a pussy. It means they aren't allowed to sit at my table, and while I hate to be a dick, I have to let my patch sink in to some of these older members. They need to know that I mean business and that I ain't goin' nowhere. I won't let any of them walk all over me since the Prez is out. "Just keep me posted. I want it finished quickly. Any issues let me know. I can send Spin out; I know he'll play nice with your crew."

"Ares," Nightmare grumbles, holding his hand out and I shake it, thankful to have his support. I've known him for a whole minute and I'm glad he likes to hang around our club more so than others.

"Thank you."

They nod and we head out. I head to the bar for some much needed liquor and they go to do what they do best, be fuckin' outlaws.

AVERY

two days later

LONDON AND I ARE BUSY PLANNING A SURPRISE BABY shower for Sadie. London and Sadie still don't get along too well, but at least they're finally civil to each other. When Sadie first showed up at the club, I thought London was going to rip her head off. She was under the impression Sadie wanted Cain, not knowing she was 2 Piece's little sister.

Now, however, its plain as day to see Sadie is only interested in Twist. He flutters around her like a crazy chicken, always making her eat and sit down. In fact, he's the reason we're planning this shower. I've been so self-absorbed in all of the shit that happened with those idiots practically trying to kidnap me, it slipped my mind. Twist brought it up yesterday about her maybe needing a few things, and he didn't know what all to get, and it struck up the baby shower idea. This way London and I can help the brothers pick out stuff Sadie would actually need and like, then she gets a big surprise, full of stuff she can't afford to get. The brothers so far have been more than happy to pitch in.

We're planning it for next month, and I'm secretly hoping London and Sadie mend fences more so beforehand. I don't want Sadie to feel bad about London helping throw her a baby shower, and I don't want London sulking around because she's not getting a proper thank you for her effort.

Ares let me know that he informed the club about our relationship. That was a little nerve-racking, but since then, the guys have stepped up the politeness. Being around a bunch of rough bikers, you wouldn't expect that, but these men have manners inside. I guess it just takes the right person for them to suddenly want to use them. I'm grateful that I get to be one of the people they share them with.

The guys have been really kind to me, so in return, I've gotten up and utilized my past Barista skills by making a few batches of chickaree rich coffee for them. They've been heading to the shop or wherever needed, practically whistling after a dose of my strong shot of caffeine-induced beverage of awesomeness.

Making batches of coffee again reminds me of my best friend back in Tennessee. He's this big blond, Russian gorilla named Niko. He's nicknamed me 'bean' since he would always have me make him special coffees. I'm hoping we get to plan a trip out there to visit sometime soon, now that the drama seems to have died down some.

"So what do you think of this?" London pulls my thoughts away from missing Niko, by showing me some decorations she found online. She turns the tablet to face me, its decorations with cute baby elephants.

"Oh my gawd! That's so adorable, definitely get those," I agree quickly. She nods and clicks 'add to cart' Amazon is a savior and a devil all rolled into one.

"Anything else?" She scrolls through the page.

"No, I think we're good for right now. We still have at least two weeks to order stuff as long as it's in the states, we should get it in time. I need a refill."

"Okay." She smiles and I head behind the bar, refilling my drink from the soda gun. I put the soda gun back in the little holder as everyone's phones around us start to buzz and beep.

The members all pull their devices out of their pockets or pick them up off of the tables in front of them, pretty much at the same time. They're so in sync, it's comical and I giggle.

Immediately I quiet my laughing when multiple curses ring out and they search the room, eyes landing straight on Ares.

He stands, shuffling a few steps to get out from his usual booth. Ares gruffly addresses the room, "Brothers, we have some company in town, and it looks like they may be on the way."

With that, he storms into church; all the members follow behind him, the last one slamming the door closed.

I look to London. She meets my gaze, eyes wide and shrugs. Damn it, I better not ask either, I'm trying to embrace these club life rules. It definitely drives me crazy not knowing what's going on all the time though. I mean it was obviously something important; they don't normally act like that when they get a message. I wonder if it was Prez? I hope nothing's wrong with Mona, but surely they would have said something if it was about her.

"Hey, do you think it has to do with Prez and Mona?" I whisper shout across the bar and London just tilts her head, peering at me like I'm nuts. She must not be able to hear me. I don't want to be loud, so anyone else hears me.

Grabbing my glass off of the bar, I head back to our table, "I wasn't going to ask, but I got worried." She gazes at me skeptically, probably expecting me to try and get some information out of her. "I just started thinking, you don't suppose it's Prez about Mona, do you? I hope everything's okay with them."

London's gaze softens when she discovers what's running through my mind, "Shit, I don't know. I didn't even think of that. God, I hope she's okay. I don't think the guys would have just ran in there like that though unless the Prez is taking it hard and did something. Who knows, we'll find out when they come out, or they may tell us absolutely nothing."

Great, just what I wanted to hear. I hate when they keep crap from us. I seriously don't understand how London can be so calm over this. She's been an Ol' Lady longer, but this would test the patience of a saint, and London damn sure isn't a saint. Ares did say something about having company so surely that's not about Mona, unless, *fuck*, please don't be a damn funeral.

I hear sniffling and turn to find Sadie walking into the bar crying. She looks around the room, obviously searching for Twist or 2 Piece. "Hey Sadie, are you okay, hun?" I head over to her, easily taking one of her hands in mine. She's such a spunky thing, but she's also very tiny with a big belly, and I can't help but feel protective over her. Hell, she's basically family to me anyhow being that I'm with 2 Piece and she's his sister.

"Umm," her lip wobbles as she scans the room again, even though we both know only the prospects are in here. "Where's Twist at?"

"He's in church, doll. Is there anything I can do?"

"I got a-a text." She mumbles brokenly.

"Okaaay."

"I don't know who it's from, but it says that Ghost is in town."

"I'm a little lost here, Sadie; I don't know why someone would tell you ghosts are in town or why you'd be upset about it." I shrug it off, because she obviously has a fear of ghosts and there's nothing I can do to help her with that one. Personally, I just don't believe in that sort of thing.

She sniffles, hiccupping and wrapping her hands around her big pregnant belly, "I need Twist or my brother."

I'll admit, I'm kind of annoyed because she's usually a ball buster and now she's whining about freaking ghosts. Get the fuck out of here with that shit. I have too much other stuff going on.

Of all people, London stands up, concern adorning her face as she slowly approaches Sadie.

"Sadie, ghosts are here in Texas or Ghost is in town," She asks, and it clicks that Sadie could be talking about someone—not a white misty-like being. I wonder if this has something to do with the texts the guys all received. It's just too much of a coincidence. Sadie starts to open her mouth right as there is a loud booming coming from the club door. It sounds like someone's wailing on the metal door from the outside.

The church door crashes open, and we watch the guys basically tumble through the doorway. They all scan the room, and when Twist notices Sadie, he rushes to her, taking her in his arms and practically carries her down the hallway. Everything happened so quickly, I don't know if she even got a word in before she was carted off.

2 Piece, Ares, and Cain all approach us.

"Is it Mona? Is she okay? Is everyone safe?" I stammer out before I can stop myself.

2 Piece grunts, "She's fine. You need to get to the room and stay there till I come get you."

"Are you joking?" I huff, wrapping my arms together in front of my chest.

Cain pulls London to him, "You too, sugar tits," he sweetly orders and she nods, kissing him and pulling away quickly.

There's more loud pounding from the door, and Ares turns to me rapidly ordering, "Now, angel!"

With that tone, I don't hesitate, and snatching London's hand in mine, we rush down the hallway to my room, closing the door and locking it behind us. I don't know what the hell is going on, but it has me spooked now.

London sits on the chair in the corner and I open the top drawer in 2 Piece's dresser, quickly pulling out one of his spare unregistered Glocks. I don't know what's happening, but he's told me before if I'm ever in doubt, to get this gun and wait. He told me to shoot anyone coming through the door that isn't in an Oath Keepers cut, so that's what I plan to do.

"You okay?" London checks out the gun resting on my lap, and then meets my gaze. I can hear some shouting coming from down the hall and it makes me shiver.

"I'm a little nervous about that," I point and nod towards the door, indicating the angry voices we just heard, "but if anyone comes through that damn door and they aren't an Oath Keeper, bet your gorgeous ass I will shoot them."

"Sounds like a plan, chickadee." London winks and pulls out a petite gun she had holstered under the long, pinup-style skirt she's wearing. I had no idea she could hide that thing under there. I have definitely underestimated her skills, and I have to stop doing that. London is one smart cookie.

We both get quiet, each trying to make out any of the words being said, but also staying alert in case we need to protect ourselves. This is the Oath Keepers MC, you don't just waltz in here all crazy, even the Ol' Ladies will shoot your ass, especially to protect their men.

ARES

All the anger inside I had tempered down, starts to rapidly surface as I attempt to explain to this Iron Fist that I will fuckin' kill his ass, him coming to my club all crazy. One of their members is outside with a gun to my prospect's head—the one who was manning the front gate—and this fucker is lucky I don't shoot them all on site.

"You expect me to be open to any of your fuckin' demands, you comin' to my clubhouse, threatenin' my fuckin' brothers? Just who the fuck do you think you are?"

"I'm the motherfucking Enforcer of the Iron Fists in California, that's who the fuck I am. You better believe you will bend to my will, or I will demolish your fucking club."

"All I'm trying to do, is live my motherfuckin' life and you wanna come into it and stir up a whole bunch of bullshit? Do you know how big of a fuck up that is? You got any idea who the fuck I am?" I don't make it a habit of throwing my nickname around, but maybe it will make this fuckhead back off some. "I'm the motherfuckin' Butcher, bitch. You don't demand shit from me or my goddamn club. I'll fucking chop up you and your buddies here!"

"I don't give a fuck what your little nickname is. I told you I'm here for two things. The VP patch dissipates and Sadie."

"You won't touch my fucking sister, you piece of shit!" 2 Piece explodes, and I could throat punch him for admitting it's his sister. "You the fuckin' Ghost she mentioned a while back? You the one who disappeared on her?" he peppers the Iron Fist, heatedly.

The mean looking fucker chuckles, "Yep, I'm Ghost. Now go get my bitch before I slaughter this fucking club."

I can't hold myself back any longer, as I launch my body at his, wrapping my hands around his throat ready to choke the life out of him. His large hands grip my shoulders tightly, bringing me closer as he propels his head off mine, effectively head butting and dazing me. *Fuck!* That hasn't happened in...I don't know how long.

Chaos ensues around me, as the brothers hold off any other Iron Fist members from jumping in on mine and Ghost's fight.

After receiving a swift blow to my ribs, I'm able to get my baring's back, launching a hard uppercut into his stomach. The force of my hit makes him stumble back a few paces, "Get the fuck out of my club!" I bellow, about ready to foam at the mouth I'm so goddamn angry.

This guy is strong and he ain't fuckin' around when it comes to hitting. He definitely has experience wearing that patch, and I don't want to see anyone experience what I'm sure would be straight fuckin' horror that he would do to them. He better get the fuck out of here or this will turn into a pile of dead bodies 'cause I'll be fucked if I let him get past me and harm the girls. At the same time, I don't want to kill them because I know a shit storm will rain down, especially killing the Enforcer of such a hard ass club. I can only imagine what that would stir up.

"He starts laughing loudly, a pure sinister sound and backs up a few more steps towards the door. I take a step towards him and he raises his hands up on each side of his body, wearing a large taunting smile. "Okay Butcher, you get your way today. I see you have me out numbered here. But make *no* mistake, I'll be back for what's owed, and you better hope to fuck that you have a motherfucking army to help your ass. That stupid bitch will be mine; hell this whole fucking club," he spreads his arm wide, indicating the clubhouse, "will be mine." He finishes, laughing loudly while stepping out of the door.

I spit in his direction, attempting it to land on him but he's able to escape it by a few inches.

Panting, I can't help the burn radiating over my face and neck. I'm so fucking pissed that I scream at the brothers, "For fuck's sake! Somebody better take care of that goddamn gate or so help me, I will put someone in the fucking ground myself!"

Brently and Smiles take off outside, as the Iron Fists bikes loudly rumble out of the parking lot. Our prospect thrown to the ground, bleeding from a few hits the dick wads left him with.

I'm thankful for our friends sending us a mass text that they had seen the Iron Fists headed out our way. Luckily there were only three guys with that dick, Ghost. Him being from California tells me that they must have already been on their way for days now.

Twist is definitely going to ask for a fuckin' NOMAD vote now, wanting to chase after them and I'm going to have to do everything in my power to keep him here. Hopefully, Sadie will be able to sway him not to go at it alone. We'll back him up; shit, I want justice myself for the grief these ass clowns are putting my club through. But for Twist and 2 Piece, this just became personal.

I don't know how long we have until they decide to return, but in the meantime, we'll be planning and preparing for them. Twist will want to lead a run to California to chase after Ghost. We just have to wait and see if and when the Prez lets him go, *and* if he's able to finish this shit away from home.

I'll be damned if I let my club not be ready for whatever's to come.

The Prez will be back soon, thankfully, and I can finally fill my role as the Vice President, rather than keep playing President. In the meantime, I'm going to love 2 Piece and Avery fiercely, giving them both every single piece of me there is; well, minus the demon inside, of course.

16 years later

"Dad! Come on!" My son's deep baritone carries through the yard as he holds the football, ready to propel it toward me. The kid can throw, who would have ever guessed this would be my life now?

I hold my hands up, ready to catch his shotgun-like throw. He damn near bruises my chest with each catch I make. I don't mind it though, if anything, I wear the bruises as badges of honor. I'm so fuckin' proud of my kid and the kind of person he is becoming. I back up about ten more feet in our large yard, set off of the compound.

He throws it just as Lily comes leisurely walking over. The old girl isn't able to chase after him like she used to. Her face is sprinkled with white, her once shiny black coat now more salt and pepper. It reminds me that we're all getting older and changing. She probably doesn't have much time left in her, being sixteen years old and all. The vet told us to expect her to live to fourteen and we're lucky enough to get an extra two years from her so far.

Tossing the football back to Kane, I lean over, scratching behind Lily's soft ear. "Hey, pretty girl," I mumble to her, and she leans into my hand.

"Guys! We have to go; Kane should already be at the field. If he doesn't get to play for being late, I'm blaming you, Ares!" Avery shouts, throwing her bag into the truck and running back into the house for something she probably forgot. She's all dressed up in her football mom jersey shirt, painted on jeans, and leather boots. She looks fucking delectable, even after all this time. I swear she just keeps getting better with age. She no longer looks like the young lady learning the ropes, but now a woman who's full of confidence and I fuckin' love it.

"Alright, angel, geez we're comin'." I grumble, helping Kane grab his gear as we walk toward the truck. We each throw a bag into the back.

I run into the garage quickly and grab a small blanket, 'cause I know my ol' lady will be bitchin' about being too cold in an hour. At least this way I won't have to say anything until she complains and she'll think it was just magically left in here and that I'm not used to her habits of forgetting her damn jacket.

"Dad, you should let me take your old bike tonight since it's my game." His dark eyes meet my own and I shake my head as I climb into the truck. Fuck if I don't want to let him though. I remember being young and wanting to just take off on a ride.

"Nah, your momma said one more year before you can ride outside of pop's land; you know that, boy. Load up in the cage, before she freaks out and leaves without us." I shut my door and he gets into the back.

Kane didn't have much when it came to grandparents being in his life, so he's grown to call the old Prez 'pops.' It's all good; that man has been everything to our kids, and you'd never know that they weren't his real grandkids. Avery's parents couldn't come to terms with our relationship. Her mom had a stick too far up her fuckin' ass, even when Avery told her that she was having a baby. It broke my girl's heart for a while, but she knows who her real family is and that the club loves her dearly.

Avery and 2 Piece pile in and we drive to the high school. Kane takes off as soon as we park to hunt down his teammates, grabbing his gear and waving as he runs off. I love the fact he has such a good life, especially compared to what I had. I made it my mission for him to grow up knowing that he's loved and that we are proud of him.

The three of us get some dinner at a diner close by the school and walk back to the game once we finish, as its closer to starting time now. I can't miss seein' my boy play, especially with all the practice and hard work he puts in.

Once we get settled into our usual spot on the bleachers, I watch the pretty, young cheerleaders going through their routines. They're all dolled up in their pressed skirts, high ponytails, and rosy cheeks. It's a cool, mid-November Texas evening. The nights are finally getting chilly and it shows as the girls rub their arms to keep warm. I watch one girl in particular, jumping around, carrying on about who knows what, to her friend.

Avery leans into me, getting cold herself and I grumble, "Christ angel, go make our girl put some fuckin' clothes on."

"She's fifteen, Air. She's going to be wearing cheerleader uniforms to the games. Y'all have had nearly two months to get used to her making the squad."

2 Piece leans in, irritated, "Shorty, you see our daughter's wearin' makeup, too? The fuck she have her face painted up for?"

"Oh my God, you guys need to just relax!"

"I don't remember seein' her face lookin' like that when she left the house and her ass just barely turned fifteen last month." He argues and I completely agree with him. Our girl does not need to be leaving the house looking like that; she looks just like a young version of her momma, but with 2 Piece's sapphire-colored eyes. I'll end up feeding some fuckin' teenage boy to a pig at this rate.

"There he is!" Avery claps excitedly and points at number 12 as the team runs onto the field, Kane leading the pack. "I can't believe he's playing with all those big guys, these games make me so excited, but nervous at the same time." The crowd around us goes crazy, scream-ing and cheering on our team.

"Angel, our boy is as big as the fuckin' seniors. You don't have shit to worry about." Kane's built just like I am, even looks just like me, but with short, dark hair. He works out so much for football, plus with the guys when he's around the clubhouse, the kid is a damn beast. You'd never guess he's turning sixteen in two weeks.

171

"I know that, I just wasn't expecting them to let him really play, being a sophomore this year. He's still so young."

"You've seen him throw, baby, that kid is the best player in this fuckin' school. Of course he's gonna play. He out throws that pussy ass senior quarterback, every damn time." Hell, he played damn near the whole year last year, once a kid got hurt and they threw my boy in there to fill the spot. I thought the coach was gonna cream his pants when they saw Kane make a catch and then launch it down the field to another teammate. The other school damn near stroked out, trying everything they could to say it was an illegal play.

A few parents glance at me, probably appalled by my language or that I actually have the fuckin' balls to admit what everyone's thinking out loud. I could care less though, they've always stared and whispered ever since I showed up to the school one day to hunt down some little fuck's dad who was tellin' him that my kid was a faggot 'cause he had friends that were girls. Never mind that those girls were his little sister and London's daughter.

Then there's the fact that I'm with 2 Piece, and that little inbred piece of shit had no clue what the fuck he was talkin' about. It took one simple visit on my bike wearin' my cut to get him to piss his pants in front of his own damn kid. Kane hasn't had an issue with another punk since, after that shit went down.

I glare towards some mousy bitch staring at me, and she turns away, freaked out that she was caught.

"You see that play?" 2 Piece leans forward, and I shoot my head back toward the field. I may have missed the play, but I damn sure notice the dickwads leaning over the fence talkin' to our baby girl.

"Fuck. Nope, I missed it, but you see those asses down there talkin' to our girl?" I chin lift towards the cheerleaders' area, and 2 Piece stands so swiftly, he damn near throws popcorn all over a bunch of people in his haste.

Before I can blink, he's charging down the bleachers full speed toward the boys leaning over the railing talking to our daughter.

Those little fucks are in for a rude awakening, and I'm probably gonna be bailin' 2 Piece out of jail tonight for assault. The club will think this is fuckin' hilarious when they hear all about it. Lord knows Avery will be chatting it up to London. They always find this shit amusin' when it comes to us with our kids.

2 Piece stops suddenly. He's about halfway down, watching as Kane and a few other teammates head over to the girls, shouting at the guys and scaring them off.. After a minute, 2 Piece turns around meeting my gaze, and we both chuckle; our boy already has it covered.

Avery kisses my cheek, and I turn back toward her "You two are such good daddies."

"Yeah, you been sayin' that shit for fifteen years, angel."

"Maybe it's time you actually believed it."

"I ain't a good dad, beautiful. I was just lucky enough to have two perfect partners and some really great fuckin' kids." She kisses me soundly and afterward I'm met with 2 Piece's loving smile and once again, I'm reminded that my life couldn't be any more perfect.

It wasn't always perfect, though. We've had our struggles over the years with many things, a big one being Twist and 2 Piece's sister, Sadie. Thankfully we gritted our way through it, together.

"Sup, Prez!" Cain greets and smacks my back, as he and London scoot into the seats behind us. They're here to watch their daughters cheer, too. Their older boy, Jamison, just hit seventeen and is giving them hell, wanting to drop out of school to become a full-patched member as soon as possible.

"Yo, brother." I nod and then grin at London.

Never in a million fuckin' years would I have ever expected to be here at a football game, with my loves, watching my kids, surrounded by my closest friends and be the President of my club.

I hope you enjoyed Forsaken Control!

Find out what happens with the club in the next installment, FRICTION, due to be released Winter 2015.

twist

Gone.

I lost my mind that day.

I arrived home, to my wife's sweet color, stripped. Her body motionless, slain in a puddle of blood, her delicate skin, riddled with multiple stab wounds. The brutality of the rape was horrendous. My precious little girl lain in the middle of the floor, pillow securely duct taped on her face. Her tiny body, left unmoving. I've never screamed so savagely, wishing I was dead before in my life.

Hope.

I've long given up on any light in my life, jaded. I wasn't expecting to be blinded with friction, by a fucking ray of sunshine.

sadie

Confused

I had no idea what to do with my life or my baby's. I trusted the wrong man, who turned out to be a ghost, disappearing, leaving me scattered. I head to my brothers club, in hopes of leaning on the only shoulder I've ever known.

Strength

What I find instead, is a hunter.

A fiercely loyal, broken man, just waiting for his next kill.

.

acknowledgements

My husband

Thank you for adjusting your schedule and the TV volume when I write. I love you.

My boys

You are my whole world. I love you both.

The Lovely Beta Readers, Thank You

Abbey Neil-Clark, Kelly Emery, Tamra Simons, Sarah Rogers, Lindsay Lupher, Wendi Stacilaucki-Hunsicker, Karah Belseth and Keeana Porter. You each stepped up to the plate and have given me very valuable feedback. I love that you can be straight with me and still be great friends. This book wouldn't be possible without all of your help. Your feedback means everything to me, especially at two a.m. lol.

Photographer Eric Battershell

Thank you so much for the amazing support and friendship you have been kind enough to give me. I look forward to our future collaborations.

Model Stefan Nothfield

You rock, Stefan! Thank you for allowing me to have you on my cover.

Cover Designer Sara Eirew

Thank you for such a beautiful cover design.

Editor Mitzi Carroll

You are an absolute saint, helping me in a tough spot. Thank you tremendously!

My Formatter Max Henry

Thank you for making my work look beautiful.

My Brilliant PA Abbey Neil-Clark

You are so good to me and I love you to pieces!

Sapphire's Naughty Princesses

Thank you ladies for everything you do to help promote my work, for all of your support and encouragement. You make me want to write even more!

My Blogger Friends

There are so many to list and for that I am in awe.

Abbey's 1-Click Book Blog, Not Another Damn Blog-Blog, Beneath The Covers Blog, Promoting Authors, Books & Reviews, Paranormal Romance Trance, Hell Mouths Book Blog, One last Page Book Blog, Literary Treasure Chest, Revenge of the Feels, My Reading Reality, Bleeding Heart Blog, La Jersey Chika Reads Indie Books, Book reviews & take-overs, Blogging For The Love Of Authors And Their Books, Shirley's Bookshelf, JaMbookblog, Emily Can Say What She Wants, Indie Impressions, Fictional Rendezvous Book Blog, Loves 2 Read Romance, Heather Ann's Book Reviews, Fangirl Moments and My Two Cents, Relentless Book Chics Ramblings & Reviews, Best of Both Worlds: Books & Naughtiness, Sarah & Kirsty's Book Reviews, Books Laid Bare, ByoBook Club, Sinfully Sweet Promotions, Book Boyfriend Hangover, Little Shop of Readers, 2 Friends Pimp Your Books, A Whole New World Through Books, abibliophobia anonymous book reviews, After This Page Book Blog , Alice's Book Wonderland , Alpha Book Club, Amos Book Corner, Another Indie Book Promoter, Bad Boy Book Addicts, Badass Bloggettes, Beers bobs n books, Behind Closed Doors, Bella's Blog, Belle's Book Bag, Blushing Reads, Book Bloggers and Reviewers, Book Bug Reviews, Book Loving Fairy, Book Talk Reviews,

Bookaliciousbabesblog, BookJunkyGirls, Bookloven Promotions, Books and Authors, Books And Coffee Cups, Books Can Take You There, Books On Fire Tours, Books, Chocolate & Lipgloss, Bound By Books Book Review, Busy Bumble Bee Book Reviews, Cat's Guilty Pleasure, Coast to Coast Book Besties, coffee drinking book wench, Crystal's Chaotic Confessions, Danielle's Domain, Dirty Little Secret's Book Reviews, Dreams On A Page, Drifting Into Books , Dummy Reads, Dympna's Book Blog, Eye Candy Bookstore, Fire and Ice Book Reviews , Foxylutely Book Reviews, Heartbeats Between Words, Indy Book Fairy, iScream Books, Jeanette Book Reviews, Just Let Me Read, K&J Book Promotions, Kustom Books & Reviews by Monica, Lina's Reviews: A Book Blog, louisemarieevans.blogspot.com, Love Bites and Silk, M&B Books Blog, MJ's Book Blog and Reviews, Nerdy Dirty & Flirty, New England Naughty and Nice Book Blog, NikiRayven's Niche, One Book Boyfriend At A Time , One Last Page Book Blog, Pages Abound, Panty Droppin' Book Blog, Paranormal Romance and Authors That Rock, Pinky's Favorite Reads, Ramblings From Beneath the Sheets, Read Between The Lines , Reading Past My Bedtime, Reading While Rolling, Rebellion and Rebirth, Reviews From The Heart, Roses & Violets Book Reviews, Sassy Book Lovers, Sassy Southern Book Blog, Saucy Reviews on Kinky Korner, She Hearts Books, Sinfully Sweet Promotions, Smut Fanatics, Southern Vixens Book Obsessions, staceyleis book blog, StarAngels Reviews, Tantos Livros Tão Pouco Tempo, The "E" motioned News, The Art of Romance Promotions, The Book Disciple, The Book Quarry, The Pleasure of Reading Today, The Voluptuous Book Diva, The Wonderings of One Person, This Redhead LOVES Books, Those Crazy Book Chicks, Trinas Tantalising Tid Bits, Us Girls & A Book, Vanilla Twist Reads, We Love Kink, We Read With A Glass Of Wine, Wicked Babes Blog Reviews, Wild and Dirty Book Blog, Wild Wordy Women, yah gotta read this. I apologize for any left out.

A Special Shout-Out To These Ladies

Patti Novia West, Jacey Jeffrey, Sarah Armstrong, Penny Leidecker,

Thai Preyer, Denise LaMee, Veronica Garcia, Leah Joslin, Megan Griffiths, Tina Jaworski, Cassie Delgado, Rosetta Wagers, Phyl Drollett, Julie Savage, Amanda Weems, Jackie Senior, and MaryAnn Comer Christopherson. Anyone left out, I apologize and I love you guys. Thank you for continuing to believe in me and push me!

My Readers

Thank you so much for making this possible for me. I wish I could hug each one of you! Hopefully I will meet many of you at my future signings I have planned for 2016.

coming soon

FRICTION

(An Oath Keepers MC Novel)
Twist's Story

UNWANTED SACRIFICES

(A Russkaya Mafiya Novel)
Nikoli's Story

UNEXPECTED FORFEIT

(A Ground and Pound Novel)

stay up to date with Sapphire

EMAIL

authorsapphireknight@yahoo.com

WEBSITE

http://authorsapphireknig.wix.com/authorsapphireknight

FACEBOOK

www.facebook.com/AuthorSapphireKnight

Made in the USA
San Bernardino, CA
29 September 2016